The One About The Sheep
And Other Stories

The One About The Sheep And Other Stories

ChipLitFest Short Story Winners 2016 - 2022

Edited by Catherine Evans

ISBN 978-1-7396305-0-8 (PRINT)
ISBN 978-1-7396305-1-5 (E-BOOK)

Cover Photo: Peter Heeling, skitterphoto.com

First Printing, 2022

Inkspot Publishing

Chipping Norton Literary Festival is a registered charity, no: 1152866.

Every April since 2012, (with obvious exceptions during 2020 and 2021 lockdowns) we have celebrated writing and reading in attractive venues at the heart of our charming Cotswold town. Everyone at ChipLitFest is a volunteer, from the venue ushers to the Festival Director. Dozens of people work tirelessly throughout the year to deliver the programme of literary events and we are hugely grateful for the support of local business and individuals who value our contribution to our community. In particular, we work in partnership and consultation with Chipping Norton Schools Partnership, Chipping Norton Theatre and Jaffé & Neale Bookshop.

ChipLitFest is one of the friendliest and most innovative festivals, bringing a wide-ranging array of writers, poets, public figures and creative people to the town and drawing large and lively audiences from a wide area. Over our history, we have welcomed Monica Ali, Jim Al-Kahlili, David Baddiel, Jo Brand, Candice Carty-Williams, Lee Child, Lyse Doucet, Guy Gunaratne, Natalie Haynes, Armando Iannucci, Adam Kay, Prue Leith, Jenni Murray, David Nicholls, Richard Osman, Ian Rankin, Tony Robinson, Alan Rusbridger, SF Said, Dominic Sandbrook, Nina Stibbe, Polly Toynbee, Kit de Waal, Justin Webb and Reggie Yates, among scores of others.

Our innovative profit-sharing scheme benefits all participating authors equally.

Aiming to create and maintain lifelong readers, our renowned Children's Programme reaches out to children and young people throughout the Chipping Norton Schools Partnership, including those not in mainstream educational settings and those who have been school-excluded. Much of the programme is free or accessibly priced at £2.50 a ticket, and we also arrange author visits to 18 local schools. Our creative writing programme for local schoolchildren finishes with the publication of a book of their work, launched at the festival.

We are committed to diversity and inclusion, and are delighted to offer our audiences opportunities to hear from those whose voices may be under-represented.

Our events and workshops encourage people to sharpen their reading, writing and creative skills. The annual ChipLitFest short story competition attracts hundreds of entries, and we are delighted to be able to offer this collection of the winning stories from 2016-2022, wonderfully varied in tone and theme, and a true blend of local and worldwide talent. We are grateful to Inkspot Publishing and to HW Fisher for making this possible, and of course, we are immensely grateful to you for buying this book, thus enabling us to continue with our work.

Jenny Dee, Festival Director

CONTENTS

CONTENTS

Ghost

I am running my fingers over the back of your hand, seeing how the skin wrinkles beneath my touch; it is warm and alive. I know every hair on your hands, every line, bump and tiny mark. How many times have they touched and caressed my body? I press my face to your wrist and as I do I feel the rough texture of your skin against the softness of mine. This, I know, will be the final time.

The machines that surround you invade your body with plastic tentacles and sharp invasive needles. Everywhere are the mismatched patterns of plasters, the bedclothes, your horrible gown. I smooth out the sheet for the hundredth time and wish it was the fine linen we are used to. I wish it was a normal, boring everyday morning and we were curled up in bed, spooning, thinking only of who will make the coffee and warm the croissants.

The machine beeps, rhythmically, endlessly, it prevents any line of thought. I wish it would stop but, of course, it must not. That is a stupid thought. It must keep going monotonously on and on. I feel that I will remember it for the rest of my life; hear that sound in the back of my mind forever.

I study your nails. There is congealed blood under them. I run the edge of my thumb around the curve of one, it catches on a snag and instinctively I feel for my purse so that I can file it back for you. This thought gives me a tiny scrap of usefulness in a world that I suddenly cannot control, but I do not have my purse, I left it behind in all the confusion. I suddenly realise I have no way of getting home and no money, but now a deep, encompassing weight has descended on me and I cannot even begin to contemplate all that.

The nurse approaches and gives me a sympathetic nod. She is small. Thai, I think, and has a kind face, but she speaks very little English. She shines a tiny torch under your eyelids and I can see a glimpse of blue in your irises. I am willing you to catch sight of me, to know I was here, but it is clear to me that your eyes are glassy and unseeing. The nurse smiles at me, with pity, and leaves and I stand up to stretch the stiffness from my body. Outside it is dawn, a shaft of lemony light is breaking from between inky clouds, it falls over the cars in the car park and suddenly, as I watch, all the windscreens are gold. It is beautiful, but it has no right to be beautiful, no right at all.

I feel so sad, so heavy, but I must be aware. I must check the car park, listen for footsteps in the corridor. I'm conscious that even now, with my brain feeling like soup, I have to keep alert. The flight is two hours twenty from Ottawa to here, they will be here any minute, I have a last few precious minutes with you.

I am running through everything in my head, the places we've been, the things we've seen. Vancouver, California, Seattle; remember the fish men? I want to ask if you remember the men selling fish in the market throwing them to each other, shouting, chanting, joking. Of course you remember them, you remember everything, every last second, don't you? It's what we had, us.

I hear the sweep of the main doors in the lobby and the sounds of their footfalls. I know that is them. I just know. I kiss you for a final time, a brief awkward peck as I lean over the wires and then I move to the other end of the ward, where there is drinks dispenser tucked away behind a smoked glass screen.

Helen is there first. She is taller than I imagined, and more striking. She clutches your hand immediately, the hand I have just been holding. There are tears in her eyes. Kierra is next, she is tall too, and blonde, so pretty, she looks just like her mother. Leo is holding back, awkward, frightened. He is too young to see this. Instinctively I want to move forward, wrap my arm around him because he is being ignored, no one is holding his hand. His bottom lip is quivering and he is trying to hold back his tears. God, he looks like you. He has your forehead, your lips. I wonder if he will be a replica of you when he grows up, I so want to know this. I want to see him when he is your age, a preview, to see if he is a living breathing duplication of you.

The Thai nurse is handing over to the day staff. They are talking about you at the nurses' station. I imagine them using your name and saying 'subarachnoid hemorrhage' to describe you and not 'professor,' or 'expert in his field,' or 'father'...or 'lover.' The Thai nurse leaves and I know I must go too. I must walk past Helen, Kierra and Leo and I must not glance or give away any clues, I must be invisible.

They are gently stroking your face with the backs of their fingers. Can you feel it? Do you think it is me touching you? Helen is talking to you; can you hear her voice? They all look so pale and shocked, so bewildered. I know I must look like that too and then it occurs to me that I have not even brushed my hair this morning.

As I move out into the ward I tread as quietly as possible towards the doors at the other end. It is Leo who turns towards me and I try to avert my eyes, but he is staring right at me. I cannot manage a smile, my face seems to be set hard like concrete, yet I feel so sorry for him so I try. Then I realise he is not seeing me at all, he is looking right through me. His blue eyes are glistening with tears, he has turned towards me as an excuse to look away from his father. Later, if someone asked him if anyone else was there, in that ward, he would say no.

I don't look back. I must give no clues, the nurses acknowledge me and one of them nods, but they do not know who I am. I am no-one, I don't exist.

I must go back to the apartment. I will have to remove my belongings one by one, leaving no clues, nothing at all. Toothbrush; face creams; the English tea; (you don't drink tea,) my book; my medication. These are the small things, like tiny grappling hooks that gave me a grip on you. I moved them in slowly, over time, but they are all easy to remove at a moment's notice.

As I walk though the empty streets, on shoes that are not meant for walking, I feel a chill even though the day is warm and full of expectancy, I am dying inside because I know that, whatever the outcome, if you survive or if...you die, I have seen the last of you. One way or another they will take you back to your house in Ottawa. I will never see you again. I picture her, Helen, looking after you, praying over your bed. You scoff at her religion but she has that now, we don't. I don't. I had you, my point of reference.

She was not as cold as you said she was, she looked so concerned and frightened that she might lose you. I rationalise that she was with her children, she was putting on a display of affection for them. You and she were over years ago. That's what you told me. She was more beautiful than I imagined too, I thought you said she had let herself go, yet I was the one with the straggling hair and no make-up. I feel my stomach lurch and I take a deep breath, which becomes a juddering sigh.

I reach up and touch my hair; it feels flat and greasy. I need a shower, but I will have to do that at my house. I have to make my exit swift and clean, take everything I can and yet, against my nature, I must not clean or tidy up. Should I straighten my side of the bed? I ought to smooth out my pillow, make sure there are no thick, dark hairs on it. I should spray some air-freshener too. It occurs to me that I will be like a criminal hiding the traces.

I feel overwhelmed with the thought of it all but I must ensure, at all costs, that I was never there. When they open the door later on they must not sense that I exist, no trace of me can be left behind, it will be as if I were a phantom that passed through their lives, unseen, unheard.

A ghost.

Jan Harvey is the author of two novels, *The Seven Letters* and *The Slow Death of Maxwell Carrick*. Both books are set in the present day Cotswolds and Paris during World War II. Jan's four years of research into the women of the French Resistance took her to many parts of Paris where gradually, she uncovered the secrets the city has tried to erase from history. Her website is www.janharveyauthor.com.

The Closed Cabinet

by Cathryn Haynes

'...and remember, the water for the tea must be just boiling, and always put in a good heaped teaspoonful. I don't want any more complaints like last time.'

'Yeah, yeah, you told me that already. Why can't we just use teabags, like a normal shop?'

'Because this is not a normal shop,' said Donald. 'This is a combination bookshop /café. We serve fine quality loose tea and freshly-ground coffee, and the customers choose their own mugs and teacups. That's one of the reasons why it's special.'

'Don't know what's so special about a bookshop. Half the books aren't even new.'

'Listen, you cheeky bugger, my customers want *unusual* books, not just endless Judith Krantzes that they could pick up at any branch of Oxfam. That's why my stock's second-hand as well as new; that's why the shelves are chronological, not A-Z.' His voice rose. 'Ten years ago, this town was full of independent bookshops! Now we're practically the only one left; so our standards are high. Now stop whingeing and get on with that Orange Pekoe. And when you've served it, nip over the road and get two litres of semi-skimmed, we're almost out.'

Stuck in the queue at the Co-op behind some old bag who wanted to know whether the shortbread fingers were gluten-free, Clive simmered. What a bloody annoying week. Partly his own fault, he supposed. Walking down Walton Street last week, he'd seen the *Part-time Help Wanted* sign, and thought: Bingo!

Big mistake.

The place was a nightmare. First all this tea-party palaver, then the endless sweeping and cleaning. Books were dust-magnets, Dennis had proclaimed, almost proudly, as he'd handed over the dustpan and brush on Clive's first day. Walls and furniture painted all over with stupid names, like a bloody kindergarten (Famous authors, Dennis had said. He'd never heard of any of them. Who the fuck was e e cummings?). Then there were all the stupid Groups. Poetry- reading, Creative Writing; they were a right pain in the arse. Groups meant having to come in at funny hours, dance attendance on them like he was some kind of waitress. Even worse, the Jazz Evenings. He hated Jazz. Made him remember when he was a kid, stuck in the flat while his Mum went to work, nothing to do but watch his Mum's old man sitting on the settee in the lounge, getting pissed and playing those bloody Miles Davis 45's. The last thing he'd done before he'd left home forever was trash his Grandad's record collection.

'You want a carrier bag with that?'

'Just the milk.'

Worst thing, he thought as he crossed the road, was that Donald was far too sharp-eyed for him to skim his usual percentage off the till. And what else was there worth nicking? Who wanted books, for Christ's sake?

'Got the milk.'

'You took your time. Pop it in the fridge and help me unpack these Daedalus Decadences.'

The way he worked was this. He'd find a shop with a sign in the window advertising for part-time staff. He'd turn up, nice and smart, false surname, false address and the false references that one of his mates would guarantee for him. He'd answer the interview questions politely, and as soon as he'd landed the job, he'd get to work. Only not in the way they expected. Then after a month, he'd bugger off and they'd never be able to find him.

The big shops had the most valuable stuff: perfumes, watches, I-pods, but they had security staff and the tills were monitored. So he preferred the small, independent shops. The stock was less pricey, but their security was usually pathetic, and he could skim the tills and nick stuff all day long if he felt like it. He'd once got a thousand pounds in a week from a small Paki jeweller's, while its overworked manager hadn't noticed a thing. Not much chance of that here.

The Orange Pekoes had finished their teas and were long gone. The Daedalus paperbacks were unpacked and correctly shelved, the box folded flat and put out for the recycling. The front door of the shop was locked, the CLOSED sign displayed and the main shop lighting switched off.

'I'll be off, then.'

'Oh no you don't, my lad. I'm expecting a customer this evening. A very *special* customer, and I'll need you to serve the refreshments. He likes Lapsang Souchong.'

Clive wrinkled his nose.

'That the stuff that smells like Coal Tar Soap?'

'Smoked, yes. I wouldn't expect you to appreciate it. You'll get your overtime, don't worry, and while we're waiting for him it'll give you a chance to do all the sweeping that you avoided earlier. I'll be sorting out the Closed Cabinet. Call me when he arrives.'

The Closed Cabinet? Now that was interesting. He'd been wondering about that big old wooden cabinet on the wall out back ever since he'd started here. The door was padlocked, and locks meant valuables.

Clive got the broom and swept round the leather sofa, then the steps leading down to the body of the shop. Sweeping the dust out of sight under the tables, he turned over plans in his mind. He knew padlocks; that one would need more than a hairpin to open it. He could manage it tonight. Nip in with the duplicate key that Dennis didn't know he'd had made, and get to work. He hadn't intended to bust the cabinet for some time yet; but if it had stuff worth selling in it; well. Besides, he'd had enough of this dump. Yes, why not try it tonight...?

'Ahem.'

Jesus!

Standing in the shadows by the closed door was a tall old man. He wore a long black overcoat with an astrakhan collar. A worn leather satchel hung from his right shoulder.

'Did I startle you? My apologies.'

How the hell did he get into the shop? Didn't hear him open the door. Couldn't have opened the door. Saw Donald lock it.

'If you would be good enough to inform your master that Dr. Hesselius has arrived?'

Then the old man wasn't by the door anymore but standing right in front of him. Bald head, tufty white eyebrows, beaky nose, and a smile with sticky-out teeth. The broom slipped from Clive's fingers. His mouth felt dry.

How can he move so *fast?*

The old man bent down, picked up the broom, and propped it gently against one of the chairs. 'Butterfingers...'

Don't let him touch me. If he touches me I'll piss myself.

'Long time no see, Doc!'

Oh, thank Christ.

'Donald, my dear boy! Always a pleasure.'

Clive stepped aside as Donald exchanged back-slaps with his guest.

'Didn't have too far to come, I hope?'

'I took the Bodleian short-cut, so no, not too far. I'm afraid that I gave your charming young assistant rather a start.'

'He was probably sweeping the dust under the tables again,' said Donald. 'Clive, the Lapsang's all ready in the kitchen, and there's some farmhouse cheddar and a tin of Bath Olivers on the counter. Get cracking. Just boiling, remember; and clean plates this time.'

More bloody waitressing. Clive sullenly ferried the tea-things to and fro, while the young man and the old sat on the sofa and chatted.

'Seen anything of Jack Torrance lately ?'

'Alas, no. I gather he still struggles with his Writer's Block. I bumped into Pierre Menard the other day. He insisted on reading me his new chapter of the *Quixote*.'

'Oh dear. He's started writing it again, then?'

'As always. Mm! Scrumptious cheddar!'

After about half an hour, finishing the washing-up and half-listening to the conversation in the shop, Clive heard Doctor Hesselius say: 'And now; to business.'

'Washing-up's all done; I'm off now,' he called.

'Don't be late tomorrow; we'll need to get ready for the Sharkspark Story-Tellers.' Donald called back.

'No worries.'

He slammed the back door loudly, then crept silently out of the kitchen and into the shadows behind the central book-case. They'd moved down to the body of the shop and were sitting at the big wooden table.

'Have you got the first edition?' Donald was asking.

First editions were supposed to be valuable, weren't they?

'Have *you* got the scroll?'

'Right here.'

Donald placed a long cardboard roll on the table. The old man took a slim hardback with a worn cloth binding out of his satchel, and slid it across the table towards his host. Donald picked it up, and began to examine it carefully with a magnifying-glass.

'Hmm... bit foxed... spine's broken...but that signature's

genuine, and the publication date's right.' He laid down book and glass. 'Definitely a signed first edition of the *Motets of Lassus*. You'd be willing to make an exchange?'

'For the Scroll, most assuredly.'

Donald slipped a scroll of parchment out of the cardboard roll. He laid it on the table as Dr. Hesselius pulled on a pair of white cotton gloves.

'Better safe than sorry, eh?' the old man grinned, and carefully unrolled the scroll. It was covered with columns of scribbly letters in reddish-brown ink. Clive was standing too far away to make out what was written, but he thought it looked nasty; as if it was written about nasty things. A sweety-sick, perfumed smell drifted up; it reminded him uncomfortably of being dragged off to church at Christmas by his Mum.

Doctor Hesselius smoothed the scroll lovingly with his gloved hands. 'It is indeed *The Al-Azif* of the Mad Arab Abdul Al-Hazred! A manuscript edition of that mighty work, in the original Arabic. Remark the beauty of the calligraphy, my dear Donald! Written in the blood of Circassian virgins, if I am not mistaken?'

'Yup. Took me a lot of trouble to get that scroll.'

'I do not doubt it. And you would be willing to exchange this priceless text for the Lassus?

'Hell, yes. I've been searching for that pamphlet for ages. Just what I need to complete the Victorian part of my collection.'

'Then we have an accord.'

Hesselius rolled up the scroll, returned it to its container, and slipped off his gloves. As the two men shook hands solemnly, Clive stole out to the kitchen and snuck out by the back door, closing it silently behind him.

Gripping the handle of the torch between his teeth, Clive positioned the blades of the bolt-cutter, and brought its handles together with a snap. The padlock fell to the floor with a clunk, and the door of the Closed Cabinet swung slowly open. Three shelves were visible in the wavering light, tight with books. Brilliant! He started to stuff them into the big army-surplus rucksack. Some were small as birthday cards, some thick and heavy as paving slabs. If all these were signed first editions, he was onto a nice little earner. When the Cabinet was empty, he slipped the bolt-cutters inside the rucksack, zipped it up, and swung it onto his shoulder. Funny how light it felt.

Time to go. He took the torch out of his mouth, and stepping out into the shop, shone it round. Why not crack the till before he left? Just so's he could imagine Donald's face when he found it tomorrow morning. Lovely.

The torchlight was flickery; batteries must be low. He snapped off the torch and slipped it into his pocket. No harm in putting on the shop light for a tick; nobody would notice it at 2.30 in the morning, and it would be easier to count the cash. He stretched out his hand through the darkness to find the light-switch... and touched another hand.

'Allow me.'

A click, a glow of light, and Doctor Hesselius was standing beside him. Clive made a croaking noise.

'Pray don't mention it.'

He backed away and stumbled down the step, the old man following.

'You keep late hours, young man.' he remarked, raising tufty eyebrows. 'A spot of overtime, perchance?'

'I'm - I'm stock-taking.'

'How very conscientious. I'm sure Donald will be most impressed.'

'Got to go now. Got to be in early tomorrow-'

'And you need your eight hours. But need you leave quite so soon? Stay for a little chat, do.'

Clive swallowed. 'OK, yeah; just for a bit.'

He's only an old git. I can get out of this. I'm young. I'm fast. I can do it.

Hesselius sat down on the leather sofa.

'Well, isn't this nice?' he beamed, and steepling his finger-tips, fixed Clive with a penetrating gaze. 'Tell me; do you *like* working in a bookshop?'

Clive shrugged. 'It's all right.'

I fucking hate it.

'You should deem it a privilege,' said the old man solemnly. 'Consider the great bookshops and libraries of the world. Consider their contents. All those philosophies, histories, biographies, comedies and tragedies, thoughts and dreams, loves and hates; chained in words and crammed into the small space between the covers of a book. After a while, these books will begin to affect the dimension that surrounds them. The late lamented Mr Pratchett dubbed this dimension *L-space*.'

What the fuck's he wittering on about?

'The effects vary,' the Doctor continued. 'A department

that exists one day will cease to exist the next, and vice versa. A shelf that only seems to continue for a few feet will, if browsed incautiously, stretch on in perpetuity. The fictional characters within the books are affected, too, often attaining their own reality. I myself started life in a collection of short stories by Sheridan LeFanu. Last week, as it happens,' he chuckled, 'I was passing through The Murder and Mayhem Bookshop in Hay-on-Wye, and chanced to bump into my respected colleague Dr. Van Helsing. We had a lively debate as to which of our creators, LeFanu or Mr. Stoker, originated the figure of the Psychic Detective!' He paused. 'Do you follow me?'

Clive nodded vigorously.

Humour him, humour him.

'Some characters' personalities even change and develop in this wondrous dimension. Did you know that Hamlet and Ophelia are happily married and running the Philosophy section of an academic bookstore near Wittenberg University? And I was a German, until my dear friend Molly Bloom told me that my accent made me sound,' his clawed fingers hooked into quotation marks, 'loike the fookin' Kaiser!'

He's a nutcase. Got to get out of here.

Clive backed towards the kitchen door, but Hesselius did one of his moving-without-moving things and was blocking his path.

'Not leaving so soon, I hope? Oh, but we have so much to discuss.' His voice hardened. 'The contents of this, for instance.' He yanked the rucksack out of Clive's grip, at the same instant kicking his feet from under him. Clive crashed to the floor and scrambled into the corner as the old man strode down to the large table and up-ended the rucksack.

'Now, what have we here?' He picked up a book with a binding in elegant marbled paper. '*The Abject*, by Gustav Von Aschenbach.' He sighed. ' Do you know, whenever I visit the Sansovino Library in Venice I see poor Gustav, wandering disconsolately, still searching for his beloved Tadzio? So sad.'

He laid down the book and, grunting with effort, lifted an enormously thick volume, tufted with pencilled notes. '*The First Encyclopædia of Tlön: Volume IX, Hlær to Jangr.* Jolly lucky that only this volume exists, eh, or there'd be no room in this shop - or this world - for anything else!'

Laying down the Encyclopædia with a thump, he took up a small book with a cover in florid mauve calfskin. 'Ah, *The Home Life of Lucretia Borgia* by Mrs Asp. Very spicy anecdotes in this slim volume,' he leered. 'And some rather revealing mezzotints!' Turning the open book sideways and upside down, he muttered to himself 'How the Devil did she get into that posture?'

'I only wanted to look at them,' Clive whined.

'Oh, nonsense, you're no reader. I expect you were stealing them so that you could sell them on the – what do you call it? The Intr-anet?' The Doctor looked down at Clive with his toothy smile. 'I'm afraid you wouldn't have had a great deal of success. You see, all these,' he waved a long-fingered hand over the pile on the table, 'are Fictional Books. Not works of fiction, you understand, but *imaginary* books, created as part of the texts of real books. If you were to remove them from

L-space, they would evaporate, - pouf! - like soap-bubbles. That is why I so enjoy my visits here; the opportunity to see dear Donald's fine collection. That, and the excellent Lapsang Souchong.'

Fucking hell, he really is mad.

Hesselius turned away to browse through the jumbled pile.

'And here we have my little offering; *A Treatise on the Polyphonic Motets of Lassus*, by Sherlock Holmes. Brilliant brain but, alas, no social skills.' He swept the four books aside, and turned to the cowering Clive. 'All these are reasonably harmless, but then there are the more specialized volumes...' He slipped on the white cotton gloves. 'Better safe than sorry!'

The light in the shop had grown dim.

'I don't suppose you speak Latin? If you did, you might dip into this.' He caressed a book with a crumbling leather binding. '*The Necronomicon;* Olaus Wormius' translation of the Mad Arab's seminal work. Or perchance Doctor John Dee's English version would make easier reading, though the woodcuts can be quite alarming.'

'Look, OK, I was going to nick them, but you've got them back now, you don't need to tell anyone-' babbled Clive.

Hesselius wasn't paying attention. He had picked up a book with a luridly-coloured cartoon cover. It looked rather like an old-fashioned children's annual, thought Clive. Then he saw the cartoons close up, and felt faint.

'And here we have *The Bumper Fun Grimoire*! A most amusing tome; unless, of course, one is careless enough to read one of the formulæ aloud. Then, oh dearie me; the same rabbit from the same top-hat, over and over again, for all eternity...'

Clive slid out of the corner, along the wall. His hand touched metal. He looked down. The bolt-cutter! It must have rolled onto the floor when the rucksack was emptied. He glanced up at Hesselius, who had turned away, absorbed in yet another book, with an unlettered cover of black watered silk. Slowly he rose to his feet, the bolt-cutter gripped in his right hand.

'My old friend Ludvig Prinn's masterwork,' the old man was murmuring. 'What happy memories it inspires...'

Clive crept towards him. One good whack should do it. Then offski, and on the first coach to London, before the shop was even opened. Find a dealer, flog the books, easy. One good whack. He raised his arm.

'Oh, no; I don't think so!'

Hesselius was standing behind him. He grabbed Clive's right wrist in his gloved hand and gave it a sharp twist. Clive yelped and dropped the bolt-cutter. He screeched as his arm was yanked into an agonizing half-nelson, and he was propelled towards the book-laden table.

'I did so hope to avoid violence,' said Hesselius's soft voice in his ear. 'But if you were intending to brain a helpless old man-' he tightened his hold, and Clive whimpered in pain, 'well, I think self-defence allowable. Pray be seated.'

He thrust his prisoner down on to one of the chairs in front of the large table. The black silken book lay open on its surface. Pinning Clive in the chair with one hand, Hesselius used the other to flick through the leaves. They were pure black, covered with a fiery scarlet script. Clive sobbed as the letters writhed and wriggled on the pages before him.

Can't look away. Can't look away.

'The greatest book of demonic invocations ever written: *De Vermis Mysteriis.*' Doctor Hesselius said reverently. 'Englished, *The Mysteries of the Worm*. Now then, young man,' his voice dropped to a whisper. 'Read it.'

Donald crumpled the courteous note of explanation and apology which he'd found waiting for him when he'd opened the shop. He chucked it, with bad-tempered accuracy, into the wastepaper basket. Damn. Now he had no-one to help him serve the drinks to the Sharksparks that evening. He glared at the pile of worms on the seat of the chair in front of him. They writhed slowly, languid and sated, then as he watched, crumbled into a small pile of ash. Oh, great.

He stomped off to the kitchen, and began to look under the sink for the dustpan-and-brush.

Cathryn Haynes read English at St Hilda's College, Oxford, back in the mists of time. She is interested in ghost stories, folklore and mythology, which she uses as inspiration for her fiction. She lives alone with two cats and about two thousand books.

Below The Line

by Jane Buffham

The most important thing to bear in mind about a successful suicide attempt is that you don't want to overplay your hand, and actually end up dead. To be or not to be is not the question when you don't intend to kill yourself. Who really wants to die when push comes to shove, however crappy life can be? It's against our natural instincts. Those who survive hurling themselves off the Humber Bridge report feeling massive regret during the fall. No one ever says they're not relieved when they wake up after all.

What matters here, Jacqui, is what this looks like.

The anonymous followers who click the 'Like' button under every single blog entry, I get them, I do. Signalling compassion has never been easier or cheaper, and when you're the mother of a dead daughter they click and double click to show their humanity. Don't take the piss though, Jacqui, their loyalties are fragile.

There's a delicate gentility to pills, I see that, but the danger of miscalculation makes them risky. Too few, too half-hearted, and it won't likely be forgiven. There might be a chorus of *there-there* to your face, but even you won't fail to notice when people avoid you in Waitrose, or stop answering invitations to your bi-monthly supper club evenings, or won't make eye contact down at the Conservative Association.

And if that feverish mob who clickety-click their admiration on your bloody website should ever pivot their digital pitchforks against you, then God help you.

What this needs to look like is a woman driven to the brink only to be saved at the last moment by something approaching divine intervention. That will rally support. They will be outraged on your behalf, ready for your call to arms.

But if they think you're manipulating them with a grisly self-serving soap opera, then fuck compassion, *you callous, attention-seeking cow.* They'll string you up from your own blogposts. There's nothing more brutal than an army in mutiny against its general.

But then again. Too many pills, and there's no coming back. Believe me, you don't want to make your final appearance in this life covered in urine and vomit while people around you scream and yell, and tear your clothes off. With your tits hanging out as the neighbours look on. While my dad stands there crying, for Christ's sake.

There's nothing more mortifying than being both the corpse and the suspected killer in your own police procedural. The rozzers crawling through the debris of your life looking for clues as to *why*. Looking through your diary, your emails, your internet search history. The finger-tip search of your knicker drawer to find where the corruption leaked in.

They peer into the vagina and anus searching for clues as

to who you've been fucking– and when and how – before removing your organs one by one. They report on the undigested pieces of your last supper they fished out of the stomach, and scour the liver and kidneys for tell-tale signs of drink and drugs. They weigh the heart as if that will tell them what was in it to cause you to stop it from beating.

If you're unlucky, someone will publish all the gory findings on a Reddit thread to service the curiosity and speculation of strangers who debate in circular logic as to whether it was suicide or a murder covered up by incompetent police.

The beginning of the end of us came when a family from London moved into our patch of suburban utopia. Him, an academic and an occasional contributor to the *New Statesman*. She was something or other in the media, and her teenage son was the product of a previous relationship she'd had with a handsome Nigerian actor. You hated them on sight, naturally. The day they erected a Vote Labour sign on the front lawns of your leafy Tory universe, you saw a declaration of war. In fewer than 140 characters, you declared them mortal enemies. *Not content with their SMUG Islington bubble, now swarms of the loony left PC brigade are INVADING here!* Fifty-five angry-faced emoticons shared your outrage.

Ollie Roberts was in Year 11, two years below me, and still forced to wear the uniform of the lower school. At first, I never saw him or spoke to him since upper sixth girls, sophisticated with our cars and clothes and older boyfriends, were practically a different species. But then one rain-lashed morning early in the autumn term as I sat queued in a line of traffic, I saw him at a bus stop huddled in a shop doorway with an insubstantial coat, scrunching his handsome face against the storm. Something about water dripping from his long dark eyelashes into his baby-cow eyes was so adorable to me that without thought I leant over and opened the passenger door, shouting for him to get in while irascible drivers behind honked at the obstruction we caused.

After that, it became our thing, me giving him a lift every day. Each morning, he would appear on our driveway, scuffing his shoes in the gravel in time to the music in his earphones. He waited outside even when the weather was bad because you refused to let him in the house, Jacqui. You would watch him in a way that might be described as hawkish, if hawks ever twitched net curtains and tutted under their breath. Most mornings as I dashed in frenzy to get out the door, you would stand at my bedroom window which overlooked the drive-way, audibly huffing with pointed displeasure as he danced away in his own little world.

We would listen to music and podcasts, Ollie and me, or discuss our friends or the teachers at school, or just some utter nonsense that would make us both piss ourselves. Ollie was the funniest person I ever met. He could make me dry-retch from laughing. Once, as he solemnly described how lorry drivers are wholly responsible for scattering torn pages of pornography into hedges for small boys to find, an Eddie Stobart truck roared past us. Ollie wound down the window to shout after it, *Pwoar! Check out the double Ds on that!* I nearly crashed the car.

On the way home we'd meander through the back roads, finding spots on lonely farmland to stop and smoke a spliff.

We'd often bitch about you, Jacqui, about what a cow you are. About a ridiculous letter you'd written to the local paper. About your latest blogpost detailing your thoughts on Brexit or bin collections, like the *Daily Mail* on steroids.

By early summer we sat our exams -- my A levels, his GC-SEs -- and afterwards were left with glorious weeks of empty nothingness to fill together. We met with friends in the park most days, alternating the childish pleasures of grass stains and ice lollies with the thrill of the illicit.

I had never in my life been rebellious, not really, Jacqui. Even you must have known that I was not a bad kid, not when compared with those kids of your friends and neighbours whom you constantly measured me against to show up my deficiencies. I had never caused you trouble before, by answering back or disobeying you. But now, just turned eighteen and suddenly painfully aware that you had occupied my entire life to live as your own, I could no longer breathe. If it felt disloyal to want to escape, or that I might break you by pulling away, I found I didn't care.

At the dawn of one giddy August morning, Ollie and I tiptoed home together. We had got drunk and then done a couple of ecstasy pills and several lines of speed during an all-night party of a friend-of-a-friend of Ollie's from football, whose parents had gone on holiday and foolishly left the house in the care of their son. Covered in stale sweat and dew, the comedown was already excruciating. And then suddenly, there you were, waiting on the staircase as I opened the front door.

'Where the hell have you been all night? With *that* boy?' you said, practically snarling with your lipstick stained teeth.

The nastiness in your voice snapped like an elastic band on the patch of skin at the nape of my neck and raised in me a sudden, violent anger. 'In a field. Fucking.'

For the record, we hadn't been, Jacqui. We never did that.

If the drugs we took together ever made us horny, then they also made us gurn so hard we couldn't ever get it on properly. Instead, we fumbled in a hysterical pile, before laying back to talk to the stars.

You slapped me hard across the face and called me a dirty little slag. Do you remember that, Jacqui? You said if I ever got pregnant with a black boy's child, you would disown me.

That was the moment I stopped calling you my mother, stopped talking to you completely. From room to room I ignored you, slamming the door wherever I went. That was the end of us, Jacqui, and you knew that. You must have known that because in less than a week, you had filed the first report of an intruder to the police.

Sergeant Pointdexter. Do you remember him? You should, he came out to our house enough times. One time, he trod dog shit into the hallway rug and pretended that he hadn't. His reports are as blunt as you expect a rozzer to write, but you can sort of feel his eyeballs roll in the subtext.

Case #11-20197, files opened August 25, 2015.

Dispatch to 17 Rosebank Crescent. Complainant, a Mrs Jacqueline Roscoe. Advised of an intruder in front garden throwing stones at the daughter's bedroom window. No signs of damage. No signs of attempted entry. No other witnesses.

- Updated August 28th.
- Updated September 3rd.
- Updated September 10th.

Always a variation on the same theme. My daughter, the *victim*.

What happy times these were for you! I bet you wish you'd thought of this sooner. At last you had something other than your views on local politics and the evils of immigrants and socialists to serialise on your awful blog. A hundred and seventy shocked faced icons would shed a tear at every new episode.

- Updated October 3rd
- Updated October 30th
- Updated November 7th

Then updated again on November 15th, November 20th, November 27th, December 2nd, January 3rd, March 14th, March 22nd ...

Mrs Jacqueline Roscoe and her bulging portfolio of the comings and goings of the neighbours, the only witness to a serial intruder who apparently stalks her daughter on a weekly basis but leaves no physical evidence. Only fucking idiots would believe her stories.

Careful now, Jacqui.

Sergeant Pointdexter could have brought the curtain down on day one but luckily for you, your postcode is too well-to-do and he knows that you have way too much talent for shit-stirring. Sergeant Pointdexter is probably not paid enough for the hassle of contradicting you.

My dad, he installed new locks and alarms and fences whenever you asked. He did the work himself, spending every weekend adding something new. You wouldn't let him pay a professional because you read somewhere on the internet that workmen can be bribed into giving up our security secrets. Or maybe it was you that wrote it and someone else confirmed it?

My dad set up a webcam that captured nothing in six months except the occasional midnight scraps of neighbour-hood cats. He knew that because you made him check all the footage. Poor old sod, I wish he knew all I can tell him. I doubt it would come as a surprise. My dad is way too brow-beaten to call you out on your bullshit directly, but when he took up his *Daily Telegraph* and retreated without a word into the conservatory on the days Sergeant Pointdexter came to call, it was his way of letting you know *I don't believe you*. I knew it pissed you off, and I loved him for it. I admired him and I envied him and I resented him. I wanted more than anything to link my arm in his and retreat with him.

Instead I stared ahead in silence, letting you talk for me as I had always done when you told teachers that I was bullied, or all those doctors that I was ill. All those half-finished bottles of Diazepam, Temazepam and Tenormin cluttering the bath-room cabinet were prescribed at your insistence.

'Selena, do you feel threatened by anyone?' asked the sergeant one visit.

'I'm telling you there is *someone* out there *tormenting* her,' you said with snipping impatience. 'Which is why we called you.'

It was like when I was a little kid and I forgot my words during the school play and you sat in the front row hissing them at me. I plaited the fringe of a sofa cushion and said nothing.

'It would help if Selena could answer the question,' said Sergeant Pointdexter, through the agitated grinding of teeth.

'Someone drew a cock and balls in the dirt on my car the other week,' I offered. 'But I wouldn't...'

'See!' you interrupted, as you always did at your imperious, uppity best. 'They're targeting the car when she's out now as well as attacking her on our property. They're following her! Where will this end? What do you propose to do?'

Sergeant Pointdexter hadn't had the relevant training to properly investigate figments of imagination, but you were proactive, Jacqui. You had a plan.

You stopped my allowance and took away my car keys, to keep me safe, you said. You thought it best that I deferred university a year or more while this 'situation' was investigated. You abruptly withdrew all financial assistance to ensure my compliance and clip my wings.

You never knew it until it was all over, but under my bed I had prospectuses for universities in Stirling and Aberdeen, as far away from you as I could get, with the pages bent down at the social work courses I knew would piss you off. Just another few months I could have claimed my independence from you once and for all. I would have been free.

I took to staying in my room, watching daytime telly and reading, occasionally raiding the drinks cabinet when I needed a little escape. I hardly saw friends anymore, Ollie almost never. He had begun a course at an art college in the September following our summer of hedonism, and had started going with a girl there shortly after. I saw them in the street once and I pretended it wasn't weird, which made it weirder still.

Then one day, there was a violent knock on our front door. Not ringing the bell first, but straight to hammering on the wood with a fist. Ollie was steaming with a rage I had never seen in him before.

'Your fucking mother is accusing me of *stalking* you.'

The rozzers had been round, he said, to warn him 'off'. And he was receiving threats on his Facebook wall. People he didn't know were calling the house.

'You and your mother need to leave me the fuck alone,' he shouted as walked away. 'You're a pair of psychos.'

The moment of my actual death was never as awful as that.

The problem with continuing drama, Jacqui, is that each episode has to be greater than the last otherwise the audience loses interest. No loyalty, see.

Enthusiasm dwindled for the stalker story until you came up with a drip-feed of clues to point to a 'culprit' for a legion of armchair detectives to solve. No names, not at first, but the more astute among your base could identify the Roberts' house on Google maps and forward on their sentiments in jiffy bags of dog turds.

Then this gift, caught on my dad's surveillance tape. The chief suspect in your imagined crime, appearing on our doorstep, yelling at his victim. There's no sound, because you made sure it was turned it off before uploading, but it's clear to the thousands of viewers on the internet that this is proof a nasty bully boy is tormenting your lovely daughter. Someone posts that they can lip read, and that they clearly can see him say 'I will kill her'. You cite this again and again and again because you know if you say things enough times, people will believe it and it becomes the truth.

I see you there right now, Jacqui, counting out pills, working out how many you'll need and what time my dad'll be home to run you to safety. I wonder if you took such care when you counted them out for me. When you crushed them into your opened bottle of Pinot Grigio that you knew I would pinch from the fridge, I wonder did you intend for me to die just so you could write about it on your blog?

By the time the coroner ruled my death was a 'suicide', since there being no evidence of any break-in or third party involvement, and given my history of mental illness (all those doctor visits and antidepressants) and reports of my stalking torment (Sergeant Pointdexter takes to the stand), your conspiracies have taken on a life of their own amongst your followers.

But the stalking.
The video.
The threat.

The mother of a stalked daughter is trumped by the mother of a dead daughter, but a mother of a murdered daughter denied justice trumps them all.

The pain of losing my daughter while her killer walks free.

Hit 'Post'.

I'll be reunited with my angel forever.

What monster could do this to her!

I forgive my daughter's killer.

So brave, Jacqui. We stand with you.

Oliver Roberts, I forgive you, I just ask that you get the help you need.

Release the hounds.

Jane Buffham has a master's degree in creative writing from the University of Winchester. She currently works for a creative design studio based in Brighton. In real life, she's quite nice, if a bit sweary.

Refuge

by Becky Sheaves

Mum feels sorry for the migrants, so she has put us on a list to take a refugee into our house. Andrew is predictably steaming, the old fascist: 'So you'd invite some, some Islamic nutter, could be a criminal, totally different culture, into our home would you?' he rants on, but with just a little twinkle in his eye that is his weakness. No matter how mental she is, he almost always indulges her.

'These are PEOPLE, Andrew,' Mum argues back. 'Human beings. There but for the grace of God. We need to reach out to them, show our common humanity, make a few sacrifices ourselves...'

At which Patrick pipes up: 'They can have my room, Mummy,' and Mum and Andrew go all smiley and proud-parenty. No one asks me or Roger what we think. Roger is busy tipping his chair and putting his peas into rows, just seeing if the debate will get him out of eating anything green.

'Anyway,' says Mum, getting off her high horse for a nano-second. 'I felt I had to do *something* about the refugee crisis and saying we'd have one to stay was...'

'Just about the most showy-off thing you could think of?' I mutter, getting to my feet to clear the table.

'Thank you, Niamh,' says Andrew. 'No need to disrespect your mother. But yes, a refugee in the house, Maura, will come here over my dead body.'

And so it was that Ahmed came to stay.

It was weeks later, a couple of months even, and we were in the dark days of November and had forgotten all about Mum's mad gesture. I was telling Mum I had S.A.D. and wanted a special light box to counteract it. She first tried to laugh at me, then looked all serious and told me she couldn't afford one. 'You want a bit more daylight?' Andrew boomed as he pulled on his boots. 'Come and give me and Patrick a hand checking the sheep.' No way, thank you very much, I think. I'm not stumbling around the fields at 7am getting my hair all damp before school.

I watched them roar off out of the yard, the dog balancing on a mudguard, Patrick beaming as he sat on Andrew's lap and revved the quad himself.

The next minute there was a sharp exclamation from Mum as she peered short-sightedly at her phone. 'Oh my GOD,' she shrieked. 'What?' I said, presuming that it was another massive water bill.

Mum looked up with a face that's half guilty, half laughing: 'They've found us a refugee. In fact, two. Andrew's going to kill me.'

They arrived on a Sunday evening. We were all watching Antiques Roadshow and shouting out the valuations.

'Clarice Cliff! £500!' says Mum.

'In that case, I chucked out a couple of grand's worth when we cleared Aunty Gillian's house,' says Andrew. They're enjoying themselves. I'm sitting near the wood-burner, keeping it burning perfectly. Patrick's in his dinosaur pyjamas trying to dodge bedtime between Andrew and mum on one sofa and Roger is hunched over Andrew's iPad on the other one.

Mum and Andrew have taken his laptop away so he can spend some family time with us, which is working perfectly, of course.

'Don't you download any viruses onto my iPad!' says Andrew glancing across at him.

'I'm watching Huahwi doing a live stream from New York,' Roger replies, as if that explained everything.

There is a knock on the front door.

'They're here!' Mum leaps to her feet, then looks at Andrew. 'Press Record on that. Come on, we can watch it later.'

We all troop into the kitchen and there, blinking in the light, is a dark man with a neat beard and a hooked nose like a pirate. Carrying a small child, a little girl with tangled ringlets and huge brown eyes. Beside them is Bea, the social worker. For a second, we line up opposite them: Mum in her tight jeans and fluffy Joules socks, hair up in a scrunchie. Andrew in a sweater with holes in the elbows, Patrick, the dog, and me. Roger hasn't moved from the iPad. There is a moment's silence, and then Andrew breaks it: 'Come in, come in! Let's put the kettle on, sit down everyone!'

We've been told not to shake hands with him as it could be culturally insensitive but he smiles - brilliant white - shifts the little girl to his other hip and says in accented English:

'Thank you very much for having us, I appreciate your hospitality,' stretching out a hand first to Andrew, then Mum, then Patrick. Then me, last of all. His hand is smooth and warm, a beautiful colour compared to mine, which is pale and freckly.

'Go and get Roger,' hisses Mum as she faffs about with the mugs and Andrew pulls out chairs for Bea and Ahmed to sit on.

I saunter back into the sitting room. 'Come and say hello,' I say to Roger, who is still on the iPad, and now wearing headphones, too. Sometimes you can get through to him with just a nice quiet approach. This wasn't one of those times. So I pull a headphone out of his ear: 'Go into the kitchen NOW,' I say. 'Or I will get Andrew.' Roger wails like a baby but I slam a hand across his mouth. 'They're here. Don't embarrass us. Get in there, say hello and then you can be back on this in three minutes.'

I shove him off the sofa, put the iPad on the top shelf and stand in front of it looking fierce. He shambles off to say hello, looking at his toes and I follow behind. Ahmed looked at him a bit curiously but Roger didn't notice as he doesn't like looking new people in the eye, not being over-fond of random strangers at the best of times. Which I suppose, to him, this wasn't.

I woke up in the middle of the night to the sound of a small child crying. For a second I thought I was back in primary school when Patrick was little. Then I realised it must be Ahmed's baby. She was called Muneera, which had slightly made Andrew and Patrick smirk because it sounds like manure. I don't know which of them is more immature.

Down in the kitchen, I found him, pacing up and down with the little girl in his arms. 'Does she want some hot milk?' I said, remembering the nights when Patrick would wail 'milky' at 3am and Mum was so tired. We even still had a couple of his old sippy cups. I rinsed one out and microwaved some milk, giving it a good shake in case of hot spots. Used to do it quite a lot when Patrick was smaller.

'Thank you,' he said, looking grey and tired. 'You're very kind, er...'

'Niamh,' I said. 'It's an Irish name. You spell it like this, but pronounce it Neave,' I said, writing my name on the back of an envelope on the kitchen table.

Muneera sipped on the milk, her chest still rising and falling with hiccupy sobs. A big fat tear stood like a bead on her cheek. I really wished I wasn't wearing a ridiculous rosebud flowered onesie, but our house is so cold at night.

'My mum is from Ireland, you see. So that's why we have Irish names like Maura and Patrick and Niamh,' I said.

Ahmed smiled at me and his eyes glinted in the dim light. 'My wife chose my daughter's name,' he said. 'That is why our daughter is called Muneera.'

'It's a beautiful name,' I lied. 'She's a beautiful little girl.' That was the truth.

'Thank you. And are Andrew and Roger also Irish names?'

'No, they're English names. Andrew is Roger's dad. Then my mum and Roger's dad got married and they had Patrick together.'

Silence. 'We're a complicated family.'

'And your father?'

'I don't see him very often.'

'But you have Andrew as a father now.'

'Mmm... Yes. Sort of.'

'Or maybe you miss your real father?'

A long pause and then I just nodded my head. 'Yep.'

He smiled again. 'You are very brave, I think.'

It was only when I got back to bed that it crossed my mind to wonder where his wife, Muneera's mum, was now.

In the morning, I came down to find Ahmed and Muneera at the table eating toast and jam, while Mum made small talk and Andrew was hopping from foot to foot before finally coming right out with it. 'Ahmed, mate, d'ya mind if I fry up a bit of bacon? I've been up since five and it's hungry work, farming.'

Andrew is like a Hobbit. He has two breakfasts. One before going outside, and then another, much more serious one, afterwards. Patrick usually joins him these days, both in the farming and the bacon sarnie afterwards. Andrew is teeing Patrick up to go farming when he's older. Fine by me, though I do feel a bit sorry for Roger. Though I can't really see Roger running the farm. He will probably have a bright future as a computer genius. Or cyber-criminal. Mum said when she heard that a teenager had hacked into the whole of TalkTalk her blood ran cold. As for me, well according to Gemma Knight on SnapChat yesterday, I'm looking forward to being 'a virgin librarian with big glasses and mid-length skirts'.

Ahmed made a graceful gesture to Andrew and said: 'We are here as your guests. Please, do not even ask.'

And so Andrew started padding around in his great woolly

socks, frying up an egg and bacon sandwich for himself and Patrick while Mum rolled her eyes up to heaven and said, 'I'm so sorry,' to Ahmed.

Then Roger and I headed up the lane to the bus stop, me trying to pick around the mud in my new Vans. Mum had bought us both new shoes at the weekend: 'I know how important it is to have cool shoes for school,' she'd said, which made me smile to remember it. Roger, as usual, hadn't wanted to give up his old shoes, then made a fuss about having his feet measured in Clarks. 'If you don't mind, can I use the gadget?' Mum had said. 'He prefers not to have strangers touching him.' Then Mum had hustled us out of there to buy Vans in the sports shop once she knew our sizes. It was a fun day.

School went OK until lunchtime. I was sitting quietly on a bench outside when Gemma shrieked: 'Shit! I haven't done my English homework!' And there followed a massive drama, with everyone competing to help her get it done.

Everyone except me, obviously. So I'm startled when Gemma shouts over at me: 'Hey Niamh, how do you spell soliloquy?'

I froze for a moment. All I could see was her upturned face. It was a trap, I was sure of it.

'I don't know,' I lied, not wanting to give her the satisfaction of calling me a nerd again.

She turned back to her friends and I heard, clear as a bell floating over the grass, her words: 'God. You know when you think someone is a real creep. And then actually they are not that intelligent after all?'

That night Mum made conversation with Ahmed over dinner.

He had spent the day going to social services and the like with Bea, carting Muneera along with him. Muneera is now wearing Patrick's old Gap hoodie, which is orange, and she looks very sweet in it.

'What did you do for a living in Syria?' Mum asked as we all tucked in to culturally-sensitive veggie pasta.

'I am a psychiatrist,' he explained. 'I had my own practice, which was going very well, and I would treat and help everyone, no matter who they were. My wife is a pharmacist.' He glanced over at Muneera, who was intently patting her pasta with two open palms. '*Was* a pharmacist.'

There was a hush around the table, into which Andrew fearlessly crashed. 'What happened to her, if you don't mind me asking?'

'She and Muneera made the crossing to Turkey in a boat. Muneera was rescued from the sea. She had a life jacket on. My wife could not be found.'

Hats off to Andrew, he ploughed on. 'Mate, that is terrible. Truly terrible.' And while Mum and I were murmuring, 'So sorry,' and Roger was gazing out of the window, Andrew asked: 'And how did you get to Europe? Were you not on the same boat?'

'We couldn't afford to buy a passage in the boat for all of us. So I went by land to Turkey, and then I swam to the island of Kos. It took five hours, through the night. I wore... do you call them... flippers? And carried my passport and some money in a plastic bag tied round my waist.'

There was a pause.

'It was the worst five hours of my life,' he said. 'At times I was so exhausted, I thought I was just going to sink to the bottom of the ocean. But when I was near to giving up, I turned over on my back and floated, for a rest. I looked up at the night sky. So huge, so vast and so full of stars. Limitless.' He shook his head. 'It was the most beautiful thing I have ever seen in my life.'

Soon after Ahmed and Muneera came to stay with us, he had a quiet word with Mum and Andrew about Roger. They marched Roger off to the GP and now he has a referral to see a paediatric consultant next month. He might have a syndrome, Mum says.

'They can't cure it, though,' said Andrew when they told me.

'But we could be able to make his life a bit easier for him – and us,' said Mum hopefully.

They've got a big fat book on syndromes that they keep flipping through. To help them 'bond', Andrew is taking Roger to a six-week course on Friday evenings at the observatory on the coast. Now Roger is obsessed with space and the universe. When he wants to tell us about it, we have to listen and encourage his conversation skills. He talked a lot about string theory the other evening. It's hard going.

As for me, I dream of coming down in the middle of the night and finding Ahmed in the kitchen again. But I won't be wearing the rosebud onesie and Muneera won't be there. And it will be all different, and wonderful.

One Thursday evening, I put up the Christmas tree.

'Is this your family tradition?' says Ahmed.

'It is a family tradition that no one else can be bothered to do, so I have to,' I explain, and he laughs.

As I am sitting back on my heels, checking I have got all the decorations nicely balanced, Muneera is beside me, laughing and clapping, playing with a piece of tinsel. The fire is lit and Ahmed is watching the football with Andrew. It turns out he is a red-hot Manchester United fan. They are having a bit of a banter about Wayne Rooney when there is a knock at the front door.

'Ahmed! Come here, quick!' shouts Mum from the kitchen. Ahmed looks startled but pulls himself up to his feet. Mum appears at the door to the sitting room, flanked by Bea on one side. In front of the pair of them, almost being pushed along by Mum and Bea, is a tiny little woman in jeans, a blue fleece and a purple headscarf, beaming but with tears streaming down her cheeks.

'Ommy!' shrieks Muneera, flinging wide her arms.

'Maryam...' whispers Ahmed.

Amid all the laughter, the sobs and hugs and kisses, I slip outside into the dark farmyard. I have a little cry into the fur of one of the heifers. Then I stand there with her sweet breath tickling my ear and look out into the night. The next minute, I realise Roger is beside me. We look up at the stars in silence, and then Roger says: 'The universe is thirteen billion years old.'

I say nothing.

'The universe is expanding and cooling all the time,' he continues, sliding his hand into mine. 'As time passes, the whole of space will get emptier and colder. More empty and more cold, all the time.'

I stare at the millions of stars glittering above us in the black velvet night.

'Let's get back inside, then,' I say. 'Into the warm.'

Becky Sheaves grew up in Cornwall and lives at Cuckoo Down Farm in Devon with her husband and children, where they run a glamping business, a children's forest school nursery and keep sheep. A former journalist for national newspapers and magazines, she now writes short stories and is working on a crime novel set in Cornwall.

Find out more at www.beckysheaves.co.uk

Walking to Dalkey

by Deirdre Shanahan

She kept losing things. A favoured tailored dress bought in Paris. Two towels. A watch at the swimming baths. The watch had been expensive and Kaye did not know why she had even worn it. When people asked, how are you? she had answered, 'Fine. Great,' though in truth, during the past weeks, she had been losing part of herself.

In the bedroom, she sorted clothes for going to Knock. If her mother wanted to visit, she had better take her. She pushed jumpers to the back of the lowest drawer, along with embroidered skirts bought when working in Mexico City and a muslin blouse from a woman in Delhi. Thick knitted jumpers lay next to exquisite cotton tops from Macy's. She had kept the cowl necked jumpers, because her mother had offered them as if the height of fashion, which they were. Once. A fashion of safety and reliability with useful collars and cuffs. Remnants of when she was younger and living within her mother's gaze. But amongst the open spread of surrounding fields in the West of Ireland, she would be able to tell her mother about the miscarriage, a small acknowledgement to herself she should be settled with a man in the country with children and Sunday lunches. She would tell her mother about Gerard. Or as much as she could bear to unleash.

Her phone rang, battering the silence.

'Mum? A fall? Are you all right?' She sat to take it in.

'Take more than a bit of a fall to hurt me.'

Of course. Her mother was fine. A childhood running across fields and ditches had done her no harm.

'You still want to go to Knock?'

'I wouldn't miss it.' Her mother's voice was strong.

Before bed, she spread 'Visible Difference' on her cheeks. White and pure, the light cream sank in but left an unmistakable trail. It spoke of fields of untrodden snow, glacial capped mountains and saw Gerard. He had planned the trip to climb Everest weeks ago. The light winds and clear skies lasting only the month were vital for a safe climb. She saw him on the side of a mountain in a padded jacket, possibly the Aran hat she had given him and dark goggles reflecting back the surrounding light from the big sky. She saw openness. The sea. A wide bay of tides that spelt renewal. Only a season ago, she had lain out with him on a sheer pale beach in the Seychelles. In the evenings they had walked along the shore to a cove nestled at the base of a cliff.

At the swimming pool the next day, the water soothed and wrapped wet paws over her shoulders, drawing her down. She could hide in the enormous silence. An openness whelmed in, while space clamoured against chill white tiles which announced, 'Men', 'Boys', 'Women' and 'Girls'. It pleased her to cut into the water, be her own knife.

She swam as weals of light from the high window played on the surface. The life-guard, a tall dark-haired man with a slithery body of delicious gold tones, wore tight trunks. He strutted along the two sections of the baths, the lower level for beginners with shallow water and the deeper where she went.

The Rhinemaidens. Three older ladies she had seen the previous week, gathered on the other side.

' ... you really should give up smoking, he told me,' the fattest gave forth.

' ... the things she did for him after she went ...'

Kaye cut down their side, while they babbled like kids, doddling up and down the length, heads ducking and bobbing in swimming-hats. The largest wore a flower print costume. The other two wore tones of pale blue and black. They amazed her by their dedication, as they raced each other while she swanned at her own pace. The smallest stood at the far end, pale upper arms flabby like a sheet of washing. No one her age was around. Most women were working or struggling with kids. The pool held the decrepit, mad, and old, truants and deviants like her. The totally useless. She should get home and do some work.

She swam to the shallow end where the sun splayed her skin and made shadows. Climbing out, she passed two young men walking along the edge, togs smooth and sheeny. The tallest with dark hair falling back smoothly like a jockey cap, pointed to a girl. Their laughter filled the empty air under the glass dome, fulsome as a breast. The boys dived in. The girl tall and long limbed with a light tan and a swimsuit cut to reveal the fullest extent of her legs. Her muscles flexed the length of her as she walked, flicking back her dark hair before checking her watch and diving. Kaye could only hang back at the sin against nature that anyone so good-looking, could be so skilful and have such beautiful legs.

The mirror in the changing room showed her slim shape. Nothing to show. All gone. Her face was drained of colour with hair pulled back. In the previous three months a lightness had filled her as she had walked around. Until the blood on the sheets.

She had been at a conference listening to talks about the social effects of the development of the city. She had been frightened when discovering she was pregnant but was torn apart at the loss, which came sharp as a thief in the night. A new kind of madness had taken over.

At the hospital. She had waited all day for a scan, two to see a gynaecologist, another to go to theatre while women in dressing gowns and pastel toned slippers with diamante butterflies shuffled to the toilet and back. One nurse came and another. She had to repeat everything, always to someone different who did the same thing; took her temperature, pulse, blood pressure, wrote on a pad. She did not know what ERPC was, until a doctor of about twenty-one, wearing a floral waistcoat, explained. Evacuation of Retained Products of Conception. The accuracy of the words threw her.

'Just hoover you out, he will,' a nurse had said.

After she left, Kaye realized, when the nurse had asked if there were any allergies, she should have smiled and said, 'Only nice doctors.'

The Rhinemaiden came into the showers, slipping off

costumes and standing under the showers. Water hailed and stroke their backs. One had rolls of fat around her waist like a half- filled sack and another splayed toes. When a shower was free, Kaye stepped under, exhilarating in the spark and thrill of the spray. In the cubicle, drying, the Rhinemaiden kept talking.

' ...she went to the opticians ... never the same again ...'

' ...this dress, they changed it even after I wore it for Mary's funeral.'

Swimsuits lay in a damp pile at their feet. The women banged shut the metal lockers, shuffling back and forth between cubicles as they recovered their clothes. Kaye rubbed the towel over her arms and shoulders, pulling it across her legs, making her skin glow.

In the foyer, a poster proclaimed the drop-in 'Schizophrenia Group,' met every week in the Clinic next door. She could join, for she long ago accepted herself and Gerard would never choose wallpaper together or furnish a room. They would not discuss the merits of different tones of paint. Her interior furnishings were the intimate knowledge of train time-tables, platforms across the country where they would meet and strategically placed restaurants not far from the station. She had known he would not leave his wife.

She pushed money into a machine for chocolate. School kids burst through the door, with a teacher lost behind trying to herd them. They were loud but small, seven or eight. It was hard to tell, for kids merged through the years so quickly. She stepped through the glass doors. Wasn't her mother approaching, arms open wide and full, her focus adrift with small eyes like pin points of light? The older woman passed through to the foyer, the big doors opening and swallowing her. She wanted to fold up, overwhelmed by the sense of duplicity. How could anyone else but the woman who was in her own home across town, be her mother?

The next morning, the laptop did not work. She did not want to drive through heavy traffic but there was no alternative. She drove, missing a turning but kept driving. One street after another until she arrived where she wanted. Cars. More cars. Taxis. She was going east when she should have been heading north. 'Rail Freight International Parcels', 'Copy Centre', and 'Flamet Metal Packaging Company,' went by. Traffic lights. Reds, greens and golds flying in her eyes. People on the pavement, looked normal. She had to try to be like that. That girl in a short skirt, had she ever been afflicted? Had that one in the black jumper or her with trainers?

'I don't care about the past. It dissolves when I'm with you ...' Gerald's northern drawl, richly dark, settled in her. His warm accent all over when they escaped for weekends, where all her selves had fallen away like leaves.

The man at the shop said he would give the computer a run through and if it needed more than a service.

'Probably the heads need cleaning,' he said.

Yeah. Right. The head needs cleaning. She had read books saying she should cast off 'unfinished business', put it in chests, dump at sea, in a wood casket with black hinges. She would have to keep throwing the boxes out of the boat into the depths for a long time, or she would drown.

She left the computer with him, taking refuge in the new

Marks and Spencer, where everything was safely the same. Rows of cardigans and blouses, skirts, stands of jackets, jumpers and trousers across the shop floor.

'Spend what you like, whatever you need for the trip,' her mother had said, giving her several twenty-pound notes. 'My mother used to say, there are no pockets in shrouds.'

As far as Kaye could tell, her grandmother had a saying for every situation.

She bought trousers because they would not show torn stockings when her mother bent or a slip trailed. A lush, velour pair would keep her warm. They would hide thinning legs and protect against the effects of a fall, though she would not tell her mother they were called jogging pants. She bought two pairs. She would show some kind of responsibility while her mother's defences were packets of 'Honey Blonde' hair colour. They stood like soldiers in the bathroom cupboard, with the sample shade, the colour of corn, recalling her mother's youth, hay-making and brothers who had worked in the fields. Her mother used to take the canister of hot, sweet tea down through the fields, along the sides of ditches. There were meals to prepare when the men came in, as long afternoons crept by in the summer

At home, Kaye folded the trousers into the suitcase, leaving out the brightly coloured scarf ready for when they set off the next day. Outside, slow traffic hissed. The morning had started chill but the sky warmed to a pinky glow with a rising heat in the day.

The airport the next day, was all glass and light like a

department store. They boarded and found seats without a fuss but once they were airborne her mother fidgeted.

'What's wrong, mum?'

'I thought we got a meal.'

'The flight is short and we really don't need it.'

In little more than an hour they were out of the tiny airport. It was impossible to work out whether Knock was a small town or a big village as they drove to the shrine. A large pane of glass spread at the back of the church and a modern section extended to one side. Photographs of crutches and sticks hung on the old walls. Along a passageway, prayer cards rose on stands and priests sauntered by, content in their own territory. Her mother bought a year's worth of Masses.

'Isn't Mrs Garfield's son going to be a priest?' she asked.

'He's got a girlfriend. I don't think so. Unless he's bringing his girlfriend into the seminary as well.'

Her mother laughed, her face alive, eyes bluer than ever. Her cheeks blushed. Her light silvery eyes looked out from fading skin, smooth over her cheeks but ragged around her eyes. Unnervingly, the same colour as his.

Beyond the crowd, a row of taps stood, each with a simple engraving of a flower or animal on pale stone.

'Have you got a bottle for the Holy Water?'

'What about this?' She gulped down the last bit of Tango, rinsed the bottle and filled it, water falling in small fountains, washing the light away. She hoped it was caught underground and recycled for it was a shame to waste such holiness, gulps of sorrow. Tears of God. The water might cleanse her heart. For she had known the price.

Her mother picked up empty Evian bottles.

'These are better. They're big. Someone must have left them behind. You never know when you need more. Good to have extra.' She slipped the neck of the bottle under the nozzle of the tap, as sensitively as leaning to a flower, a child.

She supported her to stand until steady and able to wander around the gardens, shops and prayer centre. Her stick tapping the ground, nailed the silence.

'What do you say to a cup of tea, dear?'

'I thought you wanted to go to Mass?' Prayers or meals. Tea or Holy Water. Kaye could barely keep up.

'I think we've missed that. It was on the hour. Anyway, I'm thirsty and need to sit.'

At a table on the pavement they jostled among others for space. At the side of the café, shelves held miniature plastic versions of Our Lady and green teddy bear key-rings.

The previous year, she and Gerard had walked the lower slopes of the Himalayas. They had squatted at night in a tiny tent while with the power of torch he had shown her maps of the surrounding villages. He had talked about Kilimanjaro, the highest mountain in Africa. Explained land formations and glacial valleys. On one of his old maps, they had gazed at villages in the sub-continent. They had talked about themselves. The difficulties of weekends in small towns or villages. 'But we can conquer this. If we can't climb, we can walk,' he had smiled.

On the pavement, women pushed bulky buggies and a ten-year-old boy leant against a wall sucking a lolly.

'This time of year Spring is best when everything is coming

up fresh and new. I appreciate you coming with me. If you'd a husband and wee ones, you wouldn't be able to....'

Her throat tightened. The day broke with a shower and people huddling under awnings spread wide as arms over the pavements. Metal tables were smeared as rain splashed against her legs and bare forearms.

'...Knock this time of year is at its best. Not too warm and not too many people so you can walk even if it's not as much as I used. D'you remember the day the pretty hotel outside Dublin was shut and we couldn't go in for a drink? We went off walking as far as Dalkey?' her mother said.

Dalkey. Nestled in a bay, whose houses rose on the surrounding hills. Years back. When she had been working in Madrid and returned at week-ends. Before she had met Gerard. Before anything. Soon she would tell about him. Or if not here, later after dinner, when she and her mother were softened by food and wine.

'...It was a soft evening with little houses perched on the side of a mountain like my old home. I couldn't do that these days.'

'Of course not, mum. No one expects it.'

Her mother's steps had contracted as had her own. Her world was smaller. Shifted. Away from the wild spectacular. Ranging mountains smudged against a tropical red sky.

'And May is the month of Mary,' her mother chatted on brightly, hands settled in her lap taking in the whole of the afternoon.

The hymn came, the run of lilting notes she had loved as a child '...month we all love so well, May is the month of

Mary, gladly her praise we tell...' The words flowed like winds on a mountain. At school they had worn gloves and boaters. Mostly obedient girls, appearing to never do wrong.

Her mother shivered, pulled her jacket close, rain brushing her face like dew, making her younger, fresher and optimistic and Kaye saw the huge impossibility. She could never tell her mother about Gerard or the loss of the child. Not the one or the other. Not here. Or anywhere.

She would work at becoming new. Start again. Enjoy being out in the world. Belong and join in as her mother did, flourishing amongst other people and in new places. Kaye would be like her and other pilgrims before them, who had found sustenance and new belief; the crazy and lame, the poor and the half- believers, all who had travelled so far, so short a distance, and found home.

Deirdre Shanahan's story, *Walking to Dalkey* was included in her first story collection, *Carrying Fire and Water*, published in 2020 with the independent press Splice. The collection garnered praise from Wendy Erskine, Billy O'Callaghan and Costa winner Angela Readman among others.

In 2019 Deirdre published a novel, *Caravan of the Lost and Left Behind*, with the award winning independent Bluemoose books. She has won a bursary from Arts Council England in order to have time to write, an Eric Gregory Award, as well as most recently an award from The Society of Authors to undertake further research for a novel. In 2018, Deirdre won the Wasafiri International Fiction Prize and been awarded residences at Chawton House Hampshire and at the Heinrich Boll Cottage, Ireland.

Caravan of the Lost and Left Behind available from book-shops and publisher Bluemoose: https://bluemoose-books.com/books/caravan-of-lost-and-left-behind

Carrying Fire and Water - short story collection available from publisher https://www.thisissplice.co.uk/our-titles/phase-2/carrying-fire-and-water/

Website: deirdreshanahan.com

The Equalizer

by Anna Livia Johnston

The boy walks down the street, bouncing a ball. He has done this several hundred times, more, on the way from his house to the park and back. It's a totally unremarkable residential street, like his own, with shabby terraced houses behind front gardens so minimal they are no more than open brackets, the pavement hemmed in by parked cars. Few cars pass by. It's dead quiet; Saturday afternoon, grey and cold, and the home side's on TV.

The boy loves football but he didn't want to watch with his stepdad, who would now be working his way through the six pack of lager he had bought for the match, three for the first half, three for the second, peeling back the first tab promptly at kick off.

Halfway down the street the boy notices a man standing on a step ladder and painting a window frame. The man is singing to himself. The boy approaches and stops to watch him from across the road. He's a tall, dark man, bundled up in a black nylon quilted jacket with Reebok down the arms and baggy tracksuit bottoms tucked into thick socks, finished off by big, once-white trainers. Normal clothes, except for socks with Santa on at this time of year, which is wrong. The man is definitely not English or Polish or anything like that, but he doesn't look quite like a Paki. There are a few around here, although not too many. It's a white area. The boy's stepdad says he's happy for it to stay that way, thank you very much.

The boy strains to catch the words of the song, which the man sings over and over:

'I I I I I I like you *very* much, I I I I I I like you *very* much...' He makes no sign of having seen the boy, who starts to bounce the ball on the spot, harder and harder. He doesn't know what he will do if the man turns round. After a few bounces the man turns his head and half-smiles, but he just keeps singing his stupid song as he paints.

'Hey!' The boy shouts. The man turns round, slowly. He is unshaven and has a big – huge – nose, but is sort of handsome, like a villain in a film. Perhaps he is an Arab. 'Hello boy,' he says. His voice sounds weary, as though he is always being shouted at by boys. The boy says nothing, so he goes back to his work. 'I I I I...'

Now the boy feels insulted, or disappointed. He can't just walk away. 'Hey!' he shouts again, 'Why are you singing that stupid song?' The man turns again, stoops to put his brush down, and sits on the ladder. He fishes a pack of cigarettes out of a pocket and lights up. 'Come here,' he says. The boy crosses the road and stands nearer to him, on the pavement. He scowls at the man, to make it clear he is not merely obeying, but challenging the man to explain himself.

'You like singing?'

The boy shakes his head.

'You like cigarette?'

The boy just looks at him. The man must be mad. He has smoked cigarettes with his friends, but had been threatened with a beating if his stepdad caught him at it.

The man sighs. 'What is your name, boy?'

The boy can't bring himself to say his name out loud.

'I'll call you Red', says the man, 'For your hair. I I I I I I like you *very* much!' He looks at the boy as he sings and points at him when he gets to the 'you'. It feels as though the man's finger has pushed into his stomach and it makes him pleased and uncomfortable at the same time, like when a girl touches you by accident.

'You like football, Red?'

The boy drops the ball to the ground and kicks it, hard, straight at the man. He sees the man jerk and the ladder wobble as the ball hits him in the chest, then he turns and runs, fast as he can. He hears the man call out 'Boy!' just once.

Back home there are four empty cans by the side of the settee and his stepdad is holding the fifth. No goals so far, on either side, so his stepdad's mood is in the balance. His mum is outside the kitchen door, smoking. She is hunched up with her cardigan round her shoulders. She never puts it on properly for her smoking breaks, however cold it is outdoors. She's the one who banned cigarettes from the house, although she is the only smoker, so she is now suffering for her own rules. She's a skinny woman, a redhead like her son, with an unpredictable temper. As soon as she sees him come in to the kitchen she puts her head round the door, 'Where's your ball?'

He is still out of breath from running. He wishes he had gone straight upstairs, to have time to make up a story. He wants to tell her about the man, to tell her how the strange man had looked at him and spoken to him, offering him a cigarette, and had taken the ball. Then there would be trouble, only trouble has a habit of growing and shifting shape, once it is caused. She might not believe him. Or she might blame him. Or she would tell his stepdad. The boy imagines his stepdad running up the road, finding the man and punching him. Only the man was big, taller than his stepdad, and might have a knife. Or the police might come. He wouldn't mind it if they took his stepdad away and put him in prison, but when he came back then he, Jack, would really be in trouble.

In the meantime, he stands and looks at his mum, and she looks back at him. She stamps out her cigarette and comes in. 'I'm waiting.'

'I lost it.'

'How?'

'In someone's front garden.'

'How did it get there?'

His mum should really be in the police, with her questions. Then when she got the truth out of someone, she could let his stepdad at them. He'd be the police dog.

'Wipe that smirk off your face, I said how –'

'I KICKED IT!'

'Don't you yell at *me*. Well, that's a surprise. So why didn't you just go and take it?'

'There was no one there and… I didn't want to go in.'

She looks a bit taken aback.

'You said I shouldn't,' he continues.

'Not like you to be so timid,' she says, unconvinced.

There is a groan from the lounge accompanied by roars from the TV crowd.

'A goal down. You'd better go and get it back. Quickly.'

'It's getting dark,' he says. She doesn't let him out after dark, in case of paedophiles. Perhaps the singing man is one, with his magic finger. But his stepdad is in the next room, a more tangible threat, unless the home side can come turn the game around and make him happy.

'Oh for Christ's sake,' his mum says, but under her breath, wanting to keep it between the two of them. 'It's not that dark. I can get your sister to go with you.'

The boy shakes his head. Nothing could be worse than his sister's scorn. Although he would like to hear what she would say to the singing man if he asked *her* any stupid questions.

He sets off towards the house where the man was. When he reaches the street he can't see the man or the stepladder. He knows which house it is though, and pushes open the gate. The front garden is just gravel, and the ball isn't there. He half hopes the man doesn't live there. Someone does, because the light is on in the front room and he can hear the match on TV. He rings the bell.

The curtain twitches a fraction, as someone peers out, then there are footsteps. The singing man opens the door and looks at the boy.

'I've come for me ball.'

'Come in, Red.'

The boy knows he mustn't go in, his mum has told him often enough, but curiosity compels him to follow the man into the dingy hallway, crowded with bulky jackets and rows of shoes. They walk into the lounge, which is full of dark men sitting watching a great big old fashioned telly. It's still one-nil to the other side. Interference fizzles across the screen from time to time. They are all smoking and there are plates with food smears and rinds of nan-like bread stacked on a sideboard and a couple more lying on the floor, being used as ashtrays. They are all in their socks. The smell of men and feet and smoke and cooked meat is overpowering. His mum would have a fit. Only the beer is missing; they are drinking coke.

'It's Wayne Rooney!' says the man, and the others all laugh. The boy feels his face burn.

'My name's Jack.'

'Hello Jack,' they all say, and one adds, 'You drink coca cola?'

Another thing his mum said: don't take food or drink from strangers. He shakes his head.

He looks round and finds the singing man has gone from his side. The front door clicks shut. The man who offered him a coke is fatter and older than the others, who have already lost interest in him and turned back to the match. He counts up the men: three on the settee, two on chairs, one on the floor, plus the singing man. 'Where are you from?' the boy asks the fat man.

'Afghanistan.'

That's where the boy's dad was, before he came back and lost the plot, as his mum put it. 'We were fighting you.'

One of the others says something in their language and the fat man says, 'Not all of us, Jack. We are your friends. That's why we live here. We love this country.'

Is he being sarcastic? The boy is attuned to sarcasm, frequently deployed at home.

'Do you?'

The man pulls a face, 'Well, it is safe here, it's not so bad, but I don't really like it. The weather, the food…'

'That's rude,' says Jack, 'If you don't like something you shouldn't say so.

'That's the English way,' says the man, 'But you asked so I told you.'

Jack can see his ball on the sideboard, just out of reach. He wishes the singing man would come back.

'Do you all live in this house?'

'Yes, seven of us.'

He imagines their narrow beds all in a row upstairs, from biggest to smallest, like the seven dwarves. The fat one could be Doc. He wonders if they have any women to look after them. Perhaps there is one in the kitchen, bundled up in one of those sacks, but he doubts it. The place is too messy. He could offer them his sister. She said if anyone tried to put her in one of those thingies she'd rip their face off. But perhaps seven of them could control her.

The match is now on extra time. He hears the front door click again, and the singing man reappears with a chocolate bar.

'For you, Jack.'

He takes it and checks the wrapper hasn't been opened. He won't eat it now but on the way home, when he's safe. He's nearly there.

'Can I have me ball?'

'What do you say?'

The man sounds like his mum.

'Please.'

The man picks up the ball and throws it to the boy, hard, but he catches it.

'Now go home, Jack!'

As he opens the front door, clutching the ball and chocolate bar, there's a shout from the men – someone has scored a last minute equalizer. He slips out into the velvety dark and unwraps the chocolate bar, savouring the first mouthful before the song bubbles out of him: 'I I I I I I like you *very* much.'

Tomorrow he'll have a contact visit with his dad. If he gets a chance to talk to him on his own he'll tell him about the men in the house, and how he punched the fat one right in the stomach when he was rude about this country. Maybe he will, if he could be sure his dad would be proud of him. He'll think it over later, in bed. He puts half the chocolate bar back in his pocket, to finish off then. Or maybe he'll share it with his sister and tell her the story just as it happened, more or less.

Anna Livia Johnston was born in the Lake District, grew up in London and East Anglia and has spent her adult life in London, except for a year in Chengdu, Sichuan as a student of Chinese and a year in San Francisco as a postgraduate at UC Berkeley. She has written a few short stories and poems plus a novel for children, and has two incomplete novels for adults in her closet. Her story *You're It* was shortlisted for the Bath Flash Fiction Prize and published in Bath Flash Fiction Volume *Two The Lobsters Run Free*, and her poem *Minotaur* made the longlist for the National Poetry Prize 2017. Anyone interested in her writing may contact her at annaliviajohnston@gmail.com.

Bird, Man, Dog

by Sean Baker

It was a cold, miserable day in mid-December when Thomas first tried trapping a sea bird. He was wandering the beach, as he did most days, when he spotted a washed-up piece of fishing net. He crouched down like those African bushmen he'd seen on television, bending his knees and lowering his backside to just above the wet sand. He examined the net, sniffed it, its ancient fishy scent making his nose wrinkle and he brushed the back of his hand across his nose, prickling it with sand.

Sand was never far from his skin. He always left a silt in the bath. His mum would take hers first. She told him there was no way did she want to bathe in his sandy water. So he was always having to put up with her whiskery water, her shavings gathering by the edges. He may have been clean when he got out the bath and clean when he went to bed, he may have been clean when he got up in the morning and went to school; but by the time he was home again, he was sand-grubby, or dirt-sweat stained and his mum always said how he smelt of the sea. You were probably a fucking dolphin in a previous life, she once said. And he asked her: What previous life? And she said: It's just an expression for fuck's sake. But then he wondered what was a previous life anyway.

The edges of the netting were frayed and straggled. A gull was walking and pecking nearby and he threw the net towards it, but the gull did a little hop, avoiding it as it landed softly nearby. Thomas picked up the net, the gull head-nodding away, and tossed it higher in the air, so it would drop on the gull, but as the edge of the netting brushed its wing, the gull skipped, wings flapping, with a screech of annoyance.

Thomas brushed his hair from his eyes. His brown hair was long and home to lice and the winter wind whipping off the North Sea was messing it like when his mum used to blow-dry it, and he would close his eyes to stop them watering. She didn't do it any more. He was glad she didn't, his hair just dried naturally and he liked that better.

He sat on the beach and pushed a pebble into the wet sand. On the horizon the side view of a huge tanker sitting still. The sea was grey like his bathwater and the white horses – reminding him of his mum's ice cream moustache when they sat on the bench on the cliff when he was smaller – were trotting to the shore. He examined his piece of net, stretched out the holes as far as he could, testing its strength, thinking. He picked up a pebble and threw it towards a tern a few yards away. He missed, and the tern didn't react. He picked up another pebble and found a loose strand of fibre dangling off the end of his net and tied on the pebble. He threw the net towards the same tern and caught the bird a glancing blow on the back and the bird took off. Thomas watched it drift upwards, carried by the wind. It called, to no-one or no thing in particular, just a squeaky screech that Thomas had heard a thousand times before, a 'hey, hey' of annoyance.

He retrieved his net and tied more pebbles to the edges of it. When he had used up all the loose strands, he flung it towards the sea and watched it fly through the air, unaffected by the wind. It landed with a clack clack clack amongst rocks and pebbles and empty shells and he looked round to see if anyone else was as impressed as he was. But there was no-one.

He went along the shore, kicking at pebbles, kicking at sand, away from the town centre, hurling his trapping net at any seabird close enough, missing his target, running after it, retrieving it and trying again. He looked up at the sky and decided it was getting dark, so he turned towards the red cliffs and the path that led up to the top, and headed home.

Home was four rooms he shared with his mum in a Hunstanton back street. They had the ground floor flat and above them lived loud people, always stomping, shouting and screaming. One room was a kitchen, one a sitting room, one a bedroom, one a bathroom. He let himself in with the key hidden under the half brick by the doorstep. He put his net in the red and yellow plastic lego box under his side of the bed, before going into the kitchen and reading the note held onto the fridge door with an ice cream shaped magnet. *'Fish fingers and smileys'.* He looked at the calendar. Written in the boxes headed Thursday and Friday was '4–12'. Saturday's box had 'Graham, here, 8'. He hated when Graham visited. Saturday nights were when his mum didn't work and Thomas used to cuddle her on the sofa until he fell asleep and she'd carry him to bed. Now he had to stay on the sofa whenever Graham visited. But at least he could keep the television on and watch whatever he liked.

He switched on the oven, went into the sitting room and hit the television remote. He kicked off his shoes. Two brothers in love with the same girl (according to the rolling caption) were shouting at each other, fingers jabbing, audience clapping. He turned up the volume to drown out the screaming coming from the flat upstairs.

The next morning, he was woken by his mum pushing and nudging as her alarm sounded. He had to clamber over her and she grunted as his knees caught her in the middle somewhere. He poured himself some cereal and milk, and switched on the television. Ten minutes later, opening the curtains, he saw snow covering everything.

School was closed for the day and he walked through the cliff-top park, slushing the fresh snow with his shoes, net dangling from his pocket. He saw a pigeon. A grey-green-blue pigeon, plump. It was by a tree, the melting snow from the branches spattering the ground beneath and odd blades of grass poking through.

Thomas crouched down. The pigeon had its back to him and was pecking around. Between pecks it would raise its head, listen, look, before moving another pace or two and pecking again. Thomas stayed behind the pigeon, edging ever closer, net in cold hand, feet shovelling the snow as he slid, backside hovering just above the snow, occasionally dipping down, wetting his seat. A slow rise, one foot in front of the other for balance, clasping the net tight, ready to frisbee it at the pigeon. Thomas launched the net with a flick of the wrist and his body lurched forward. One pebble caught the pigeon on the side of the head, and it stumbled.

It was half crouched under the net, in a ring of pebbles, wings outstretched, eyes like black glass. It was making that caroo-caroo sound he'd heard so many times, though never this close before.

He stamped on its head. He felt his eyes sting when he saw what he had done, saw the blood-pink snow. He knelt down and touched the breast – warm and soft – and stroked it. He wondered what to do next. He felt his tummy churn.

He hid it under a bush, covered it in snow and walked along the path of the park on the cliff overlooking the North Sea. The wind gusted and he stumbled. He shivered and kept his head down when a man and woman walked past him. He heard them tut and wondered if he should tell them there was no school today, that it was all the snow's fault.

He went down the steps between the raised beds covered in snow and onto the pavement. Grown-ups gripping little kids' hands, or pushing pushchairs, passed him as he reached the bowling alley.

A man was sitting on the pavement, his legs outstretched, ankles crossed. He was leaning back against the plate glass of the alley, a dog lying by him, its head on the man's lap. The dog was stretched out and Thomas could make out its ribs. The man had a cigarette in his mouth, pointing down like it was stuck there. His blue hood half hid his face which was grey-stubbled and grainy like sandy driftwood. The man was staring straight ahead at the deserted bandstand opposite. He asked the man if he had matches. The man ignored him.

– You got matches? Thomas repeated.

The man looked up. Thomas wondered if he didn't understand English, so he cupped an imaginary matchbox and struck an imaginary match.

The man took the cigarette from his mouth and stubbed it on the pavement. A quiet sizzle as it sank into the slushed ice.

– You got a fag, have yer? he asked.

– Don't smoke, said Thomas.

– What you want matches for then?

– I got a pigeon.

The man's eyes narrowed.

– And?

– It's dead.

– You kill it? said the man.

– I didn't mean to, said Thomas.

– You gonna set fire to it? said the man. Destroy the evidence?

Thomas shrugged again.

– Seems a waste of a good pigeon to me, said the man.

– I saw someone on telly cook one last week.

– They're very tasty, pigeons.

– We could cook it.

– How you gonna do that?

Gulls above them yelped, hanging on the winter thermals. Thomas's teeth clickered and he tightened his body.

– Don't know, he said.

– We could share it, said the man.

The dog raised its head, yawning, baring its yellow teeth. Its nose twitched in several directions, twitch twitch twitch.

– It's in the park, said Thomas, turning his head towards the sea front.

The man stood up. Thomas took a step back and the dog sniffed around his feet, up and down his legs. Thomas stroked the top of its head.

– Come on then young'un, gruffed the man.

They walked towards the park.

– What's yer name? asked the man.

– Thomas.

– Whatcha doing out on yer own?

– Nothing.

The man raised his chin. Thomas wondered about the man's mouth and how small it looked. His cheeks and nose and chin all seemed to be drawn towards it as though it was slowly sucking in his whole face. His lips were thin, hardly there at all really, like when Thomas drew a pencil line and then rubbed it out but you could still just see it. The dog drank from a melting pool in the road by the kerb.

– I've never had pigeon, said Thomas.

– By the looks of yer, you ain't had much of anything.

– I have nuggets most nights.

The dog walked with them, tail swinging.

– What's its name? asked Thomas.

– Just call it Dog.

– Doesn't it mind?

– It's a dog.

– I think pets should have a name.

– Why?

Thomas couldn't think of an answer to this so he kept quiet.

They reached the park and Thomas ran ahead to retrieve his pigeon. Dog ran too, overtaking him, his nose leading him straight to the spot and he pushed his nose into the snow. A shout from the man made Dog look up and he slowly sat, breath steaming from his panting tongue, his wagging tail brushing the snow behind him. Thomas picked up the pigeon by the feet and showed it to the man. The man took it.

– Good and plump, he said. We'll take it down the beach.

– Why?

– It's more private.

They walked down the tarmac ramp to the beach and the man led them to the foot of the cliffs.

– First thing you have to do is pluck it, he said. You ever done that?

Thomas shook his head. The man brushed snow off a rock, revealing red stone, and sat close to the cliff-face. Dog wandered among the rocks and pebbles, his nose leading him here and there.

The man tugged at the wing feathers and they came away with a quiet crack. He pulled at the smaller, fluffier feathers underneath and Thomas began to see grey-blue flesh around one wing. The man did the same with the other wing, releasing the feathers as he pulled them. Thomas watched the feathers fly away, higher and higher. He picked a random feather to watch, trying to follow its swirling path as it got higher and higher, further and further. Dog barked at the gulls above its head and they screeched back. Thomas listened to the battle of bark and screech.

– Are you watching? said the man. I'm doing this for both of us, you know.

Thomas squatted and folded his arms, shoulders hunched.

– What's your name? he asked.

– Guess.

Thomas frowned. Breast feathers were swirling all round them and Thomas caught one and blew it off his palm.

– I can't guess, said Thomas. It could be anything.

– Could be. But it ain't. Now, see how I do this? Pull em out gentle. It's very important not to tear the flesh, see.

– Can I try?

The man handed Thomas the pigeon and Thomas tugged at the downy feathers. They came away from the breast in bunches and Thomas laughed as he tugged.

They finished plucking and the man took a knife from inside his coat. It had a big blade, shiny. The man placed the carcass on the rock and held out a wing. He chopped down hard and made a sawing movement to get through the bone. He flipped the pigeon over and repeated the action with the other wing.

– Now we cut off the feet.

He tossed the pigeon feet away and stretched the neck out along the rock.

– You made a mess of its head, he said.

– Didn't know how to kill it, said Thomas. So I stamped on it.

– Good a way as any.

The man cut off the head, close to the body, and lobbed it into the snow nearby. He called to Dog. Dog bounded towards them and his nose found the head, all blood and staring eyes and crushed bone. He licked it, grabbed it, tossed it into his mouth, crunching and swallowing.

The man cut just below the breastbone.

– This is what Dog's waiting for, he said.

He pushed two fingers deep into the pigeon, feeling in the bloody darkness. He pulled his fingers back and the slimy, blood-brown innards spilled onto the rock. He dived his fingers back in and flicked out the heart and lungs. He gathered the guts and threw them to Dog.

– Your hand's all bloody, said Thomas.

– Dog'll lick that clean.

He held out his hand. Dog had swallowed the innards in a single gulp and was sniffing the snow and pebbles around. His nose found the man's outstretched hand and he licked it clean, licking his lips when he finished, drool dripping onto the snowy sand.

The man opened his pack and took out a small saucepan.

– Fill this with snow and mind you don't get any sand in it.

Clambering, Thomas scraped snow from the rocks into the pan. When he turned back, he saw the man was walking to the snow's edge, where the sea had melted the snowfall and the beach was visible. Thomas followed him.

The man had put down his pack by a barnacled groyne and gathered some rocks into a ring.

– Are we cooking it now? said Thomas.

– Sit yourself down there.

Thomas sat on the cold, damp sand. Dog nudged him, its nose on his cheek. Thomas scruffed its head and let Dog sniff all round his face and neck. The man took a camping stove out of his pack and set it in the middle of the rocks. He lit the stove and put the pan of snow on it.

– How long will it take? asked Thomas.

– Take about forty minutes I reckon. Snow's got to melt, then boil, then we cook the taters.

– What about the pigeon?

The man reached in his pack and took out a small frying pan.

– We'll cook em in this, won't take long. I like em pink.

The man tossed Thomas two potatoes and held out his knife.

– Peel these.

– Never peeled potatoes before, said Thomas.

– You wouldn't survive long on yer own would yer?

– I'm a fast learner.

The man grinned and sliced rough chunks of skin off one potato.

– Now you try, he said. Move the knife away from yer or you'll end up cutting yerself.

Thomas swiped the knife across the potato and a large chunk landed on the sand.

– That's your bit, said the man. Not so hard, remember you just want the skin off.

Thomas tried again and another lump, similar sized, fell onto the sand.

– Give it here, said the man. Or we'll starve.

When the potatoes were peeled and cut, the man put them on top of his pack and picked up the pigeon.

– Just need to the cut the breasts off this, he said.

He rested the body on his lap and Thomas watched him slowly slide his knife around the pigeon, cutting away two breasts.

The man dropped the small chunks of potato into the pan of boiling water, then began rolling a cigarette.

– Want one? he asked Thomas.

Thomas shook his head and said:

– Where do you live?

– Wherever I want. Everywhere.

– Sounds like fun.

– You reckon?

Thomas thought about this. He thought about home and his mum and how it wasn't the same any more.

– Have you always lived like this?

The man concentrated on his roll-up, licking the paper. He struck a match in cupped hands and lit it.

– Not always.

– Why do you?

– Why do I what?

– Live everywhere.

– You ever think maybe I have no choice?

Thomas wondered if he'd seen the man before but then decided he'd have remembered Dog, so figured he probably hadn't.

– I want to live everywhere, said Thomas.

– Everywhere? Or anywhere but home?

Thomas said nothing.

– I don't think you would, said the man.

– Why not?

– Freezing your bollocks off every night? I'd rather have what you got, a place to go home to. Warm is it?

– Suppose so.

– Live with your mum and dad?

– Just mum.

– She look after you?

– A bit. I guess. She's got Graham now, so . . .

– Oh she's got Graham has she?

Thomas stared at the pan boiling the potatoes. He could feel the heat coming from the steam and from the stove.

– How do you know when they're done? he said.

– Practice.

– But how?

The man rubbed his hands together, his fingers locked, the cigarette stuck to his bottom lip.

– You poke them with a knife, he said. If the knife goes in easy, they're done.

The man finished his cigarette, and flicked the end over the groyne.

– Who's this Graham then? said the man.

Thomas dug in the sand with a pebble, said nothing. With his other hand he stroked Dog, who was curled up by his feet, next to the stove.

– Can I come with you? said Thomas.

– Come where?

– Everywhere.

The man checked the potatoes in the pan, poking the tip of his knife into them.

– Remember, I never asked you, he said.

Thomas played with the pebble in the sand some more.

– I know, he said.

The man picked up a pebble of his own and tossed it into the sand near Thomas. He picked up another and tossed it the other side of Thomas. Dog barked.

– What would yer mum say? said the man.

– Don't know.

The man continued tossing more pebbles, some over Thomas's head, splatting on the sand behind him, some landing in front, at his feet.

– You're in a circle of stones now, said the man.

He leant forward and Thomas met his eyes.

– Surrounded, said the man.

And he laughed, coughed and laughed. Dog raised his head and barked.

– Have yer got a coin?

Thomas reached in his pocket, felt a fifty pence piece. He handed it to the man.

– What do you want it for?

The man balanced it on the back of his thumb, the thumb tucked under his forefinger.

– If it's heads yer go back 'ome.

– What if it's tails?

The man swung his arm round towards the sea.

– Then it's everywhere isn't it? he said.

He spun the coin into the air and they both watched it skywards and followed it to its wet landing on the sand.

– I want a name, said Thomas.

– You've got a name.

– A different name.

Both were silent before the man said:

– Well, he's Dog, so you can be Boy.

– Boy's boring.

The man stroked his stubbly chin.

– Well yer small as a sparrer, legs like twigs. How about bird?

– I like bird.

– Bird it is then.

Sean Baker is based near Cambridge and teaches creative writing at Anglia Ruskin University, from where he was awarded a PhD in 2021. He has had three plays published by Off The Wall Plays and his work has been performed around the world, including in Canada, the USA and Australia. He is currently working on his first novel.

Ice Cream Sunday

by Jupiter Jones

The day it happened, her mood was as black as the sky was blue. But it was exactly the kind of weather everyone else had been waiting for and on the spur of the moment, they headed for the coast. Car boots hastily crammed with picnics, windbreaks, sunhats, inflatable whales, kites, flip-flops, and folding chairs. Tarmac arteries clogged to a standstill as carparks and overspill-carparks filled to capacity. Local traders put out their tat and rubbed their hands. The sands were washed and ready. Soft just below the seawall, flat and brown further out, flat as far as the eye can see, then flattish but imprinted with rippled ridges of fossilised waves. And beyond that, impossibly far out, a flat sea glinting in the sun.

The temperature soared, but an onshore breeze made everyone except their mothers sure that no sun-lotion was necessary. By the afternoon the mothers were proved right. Grandads with shirtsleeves rolled up were leathering nicely but younger men in tee-shirts had arms like crabsticks, and boys with their tops off were partially cooked and would be sore later. Girls sported strap-marks: bikini tops, halter necks, spaghetti straps. Matrons with wider straps to bear the downward force of hefty bosoms, they too would later lie in bathtubs marvelling at the milky whiteness of breasts against the brownness of arms, as if only the breasts were their own and the arms were, well, someone else's.

From the shuttered cool of her hotel room she watched all this; she watched the day and its joy. She was supposed to be joyful, blissful even, but there she was, kicking her heels, neglected and resentful; that half-dead feeling that so easily turns to recklessness or malice. Outside, on the promenade below, a cavalcade of girls in ice cream-coloured dresses, flirting, licking candyfloss and sucking slush puppies; boys strutting and winking under kiss-me-quick hats. Transistor radios shat out pop, and in the distance, she could hear the whoop and blare of Pleasureland, the ching-ching-ching of penny arcades, the raucous blather of gulls. She rang room service for a plate of crab sandwiches and passed the time writing her research paper.

When the sun was dipping towards the horizon, deckchairs were packed away, inflatables and windbreaks pushed any old how into the hot boots of hot cars for the return journey, the sea came inching in over the rippled sand and over the flat, erasing moats and castles. Then the old ladies of the town began patting their hair, selecting earbobs, spraying cologne in preparation for their *passeggiata*. Feeling more neglected than ever, feeling destructive, she put on a new linen dress the colour of raspberry sorbet and walked along the sea front.

He was leaning against the side of an ice cream kiosk; the

shutter down, the door padlocked. A wire mesh bin nearby was packed with a thousand discarded wrappers: Fab, Zoom, Screwball, Orange Maid, Cider-lolly, Funny-feet, Chocopotamus, Twicer, and Crazy-Joe-Cola. Below the bin, a line of ants prepared to feast. Paper wrappings are reasonably hygienic, she conceded, but still, the sight made her feel sticky. *Hokey-pokey penny a lick*: her research was on the spread of disease attributed to contaminated ice and insanitary practices of nineteenth-century street vendors. The man took a squashed packet of Marlboros from his shirt pocket and extracted one. He was skinny with a mouth like a frog; thin lipped with a slight downward curve; an upside-down smile. Certainly not her type. He looked her up and down as she walked past. He looked far more than was polite, and she turned away, as if she hadn't noticed him; as if.

She lengthened her stride but slowed her pace as though walking a line. This necessitates a slight swivel of the hips, something like Marilyn Monroe as Sugar Kane on the station platform in Some Like it Hot. But this Sugar didn't have the voluptuous arse. It would broaden later in middle age, but then, although well-dressed, well-groomed, she knew she was not much to look at; a bit gawky, a bit prim, perhaps already passed her prime. She sauntered as far as the pier, and along to the halfway point, a little timbered piazza where the local men were beginning to cluster with rods and bait. She hesitated, thinking of going on to the cafe at the end of the pier where they sold tea and instant coffee in thick Pyrex cups and saucers. But they were probably wiping down tables, turning signs from open to closed. She leant over the cast-iron railings watching the brown sea creep over the brown sand while the men with the rods grumbled about how the trippers were somehow responsible for the scarcity of dabs.

The pier railings were encrusted with layers of paint finishing in the palest mint green. In some parts it was flaking away, rust underneath forcing it up and off, other places it bubbled as if with an eruption of acne. She wondered if the pier would ever be painted again, if it was still loved, as if love rather than economics called the shots. She picked at the railings with her fingernail and like mille-feuille pastry, a piece lifted off, a little piece of history, of Victoriana, of seaside architecture, a piece of the day.

Then she turned and sauntered back past the glazed gazebo shelters with ornate curlicued benches and graffiti; a plethora of initials, pairs joined by + and encircled by hearts. And names of people proclaiming they woz here. She could see the attraction. An act of vandalism, a little bit of damage to alleviate feelings of insignificance. If she had a pocketknife, she could have left her mark. Her initials, the date. Proof of life, to make herself visible, to make the day count for something. She walked back to the promenade. He was still there.

As the distance between them decreased she felt foolish. That inconsequential foolishness of passing a stranger twice; perhaps having already nodded in greeting or acknowledgement, perhaps not; but there exists the faintest sliver of acquaintance, a sense of obligation, a feeling of having to account for yourself; that you perhaps turned back the way you came because you were lost, or mistaken, or had a change of heart? Perhaps you suddenly remembered you were really supposed to be somewhere else? He smiled.

'Do you have a light?'

'I don't –'

'Thought not.'

'Sorry.'

'But you came back.'

'Well, I –'

'Come for a drink with me?'

She hesitated. She really should have said no. Thanks, but no. But she hesitated and he elbowed himself upright and took her hand.

'This way.'

She couldn't take him in all at once. Fettered by shyness, her gaze inched along from the hand holding hers; it was tanned and calloused; a working hand. His shirt sleeves were rolled up and she had estimated that he was younger than her by perhaps five, maybe ten years, but the shirt was incongruous. An old man's shirt in a pale flannel with a faint stripe. A shirt that had been worn and washed over many years. She wondered if the women in his family were frugal and resourceful, if they turned collars and cuffs the way her grandmother used to, the way that no-one does anymore. He was wiry, with the strength of a coil, and scarcely taller than her. His hair was longish, over his collar, mid-brown and thin. Jeans, of course, and boots despite the heat. He was unremarkable after all. One quick drink, she told herself.

'You're not from here are you?' he said.

'No, just staying a few days.' And she couldn't bring herself to tell him why she was there, how special it was supposed to be.

'Where are you staying?'

'Hotel Excelsior.'

'Oh, very swish! One of my cousins works there, in the kitchens.'

As they walked, he told her his name was Marco, and that his uncle had the concession from the town council for all the ice cream kiosks, and because one of his uncle's part-time girls hadn't turned up for work, he had been co-opted, and had spent all day handing out ice creams and lollies, taking payment, counting change. His uncle had driven round every couple of hours, harvesting cash from each kiosk, delivering more stock from his lock-up, and reluctantly agreeing to serve customers for five minutes while Marco stood out of sight to piss into an empty pop bottle. He spat.

'It is woman's work, serving people all day, bending into the freezer and smiling, and apologising for only having what we have, and not having the Pineapple Mivvi, and the people are so rude, speak to me like I am nobody, and waiting while spoilt babies are lifted up to point at the picture of what they like, then they change their minds and they cry if they don't get what they want, as if it would be my fault, such brats, and the parents treating them like little princes, no matter that the queue is getting longer. And old people; always the ice cream sandwich for the old people, which is tricky with the little packets of wafers, and unwrapping the ice cream, and they want that I should do it for them. I tell you, it is woman's work, and they are deaf when I say how much money, and the money is in their purse which is in their bag and must be passed to them while they faff and the queue is longer like a snake, and dirty children with no pleases and thankyous, and the money, always so sticky from sweaty hands –'

She pulled away and he laughed.

'I have washed. My hands are clean. But my uncle, he is a bastard sod of a man, expecting me to cover his arse because some silly part-time little girl says she wants work and then when the sun shines and there is work to do, she says no, she will spend the day with her boyfriend.'

For the first time, she looked him in the eye and his eyes were small and dark, deeply set and difficult to read.

'So, you are too macho for the ice cream trade?'

'Now you are laughing at me.'

She said she wasn't. She worried that she had somehow offended him. She was accustomed to taking care not to seem too opinionated, too forthright; her self-censorship was habitual. But sometimes, still, she got it wrong. She thought he was angry, over-sensitive, but then he grinned and skipped in front of her, took her by the shoulders and kissed her with his thin-lipped frog mouth tasting of Tizer and Marlboros.

'I am not an ice cream man. I am in rubber. I am a tyre fitter for my other uncle who has a garage, but Sunday is my day off.'

She blushed, because in that split second after he said rubber but before he said tyres, she thought kinky rubber, and she could see by his smirk that he knew it, and he knew because it was a line that had worked before. Other girls, other women had thought the same, blushed the same.

'And you, what do you do, posh Hotel Excelsior lady?'

She told him that she was a historian, and she said it like that, not 'an historian' and that she was writing about street vendors implicated in the spread of diseases. That in the nineteenth century, ice cream men were suspected of spreading tuberculosis.

'Well they probably didn't,' she said quickly, not wanting to bad-mouth his presumptive forebears. 'But they almost certainly did spread other diseases like cholera and typhoid.' (as if that made it any better) 'Then a law was passed in 1899 banning penny lickers – that's the little glass dishes the street vendors served ices in, before cones were invented. Those old Hokey-pokey men just gave the lickers a quick wipe over with a damp cloth between customers; they were pretty rank.'

'Hokey pokey men?'

'Yeah, from their shout: G*elati! O che pocco!*

And he corrected her pronunciation: '*O che pocco*. So, my uncle, he is a filthy Hokey-pokey man, I will tell him this. And Grandpappy Joe also.'

'Hokey-pokey, penny a lick.' All afternoon it had been in her head, like an earworm: *Hokey-pokey-penny-a-lick.*

He took her hand and turned it over; was he looking for the thin white line around her finger that would indicate a wedding band? Then he licked the inside of her arm from the crook of her elbow to her wrist, over the heel of her hand, up her palm, lifeline, loveline, and his tongue slipped between her fingers.

Presently, he led her up a side street, beyond the postcard-and-trinket shops, past a launderette to a dingy bar; the sort that doesn't try to attract trippers. They sat in a nicotine-yellow corner below a glass case containing a stuffed hammerhead shark that had seen better days, and old glass floats in rope nets, and a chalked notice refusing credit. They drank and teased one another while the light outside faded and the sea crept under the pier and dabs came swimming, some of the little ones were caught, and the fishermen grumbled just the same, and uncles counted out their days' takings on kitchen tables, and for once, were satisfied.

When the bar closed, he took her down to the sands and they walked, slowly, slowly.

'So, what is a historian from London doing here, in this ramshackle dump of a town?'

'A holiday,' she lied.

'On your own?'

She was a very bad liar, so she kissed him.

Beyond the pier was an expanse of dunes, soft and shifting beneath their feet, and there they lay under a sequined sky with legs entwined and his calloused hands unzipped her raspberry dress. She traced her fingers down the lean length of his body, she could see almost nothing, but imagined him tanned to his low-slung jeans, pale below. At one point, she cried out and he stifled her noise with a hand over her mouth and shushed into her ear, her neck, knowing they were not the only ones coupling in the dunes, so they fucked silently.

Afterwards, he reached for his shirt and the cigarettes in the pocket, flipped one between his lips, but still he had no light. So they went back towards the town, past the yacht club and the boating lake and then on, between the rows of white stucco facades, all shuttered up, as if their eyes were closed. She walked along the promenade in bare feet, and the pavement still held the heat of the day.

'Mind you don't step in anything. You will need to give your feet a wash before you slip into your clean Hotel Excelsior bedsheets.' He lifted her hand to his downturned frog mouth, kissed her wrist.

'Yes, I will wash.'

They parted on the corner, he was heading to the all-night cafe, then home, wherever that was. He could have said he was working tomorrow; he could have asked her to meet him afterwards. He didn't even look around as he walked away, but raised one arm; a salute, a farewell.

She put her shoes back on before she ran up the steps and rang the bell for the hotel night porter to let her in. The place *was* rather grand with its marble tiled floors, enormous gilt framed mirrors and liveried staff.

'Ah, Missus Stephens,' said the porter, 'I hope you had a pleasant walk. A little stroll along the sea front is the very thing when one cannot sleep on these hot sticky nights. And I have just, not ten minutes since, welcomed your husband back. He said the golf tournament at the Royal Birkdale went well, very well indeed, he was more than a bit tipsy. And . . . well . . . *goodnight* Missus Stephens.'

She thanked him and made her way upstairs, fingering in her pocket a fragment of the pier balustrade, rusted iron flake on one side, palest mint-green on the other.

Jupiter Jones lives in Wales and writes short and flash fictions. She is the two-time winner of the Colm Tóibín International Prize, and her stories have been published by Aesthetica, Brittle Star, Fish, Scottish Arts, and Parthian. Her first novella-in-flash, *The Death and Life of Mrs Parker* was published by Ad Hoc Fiction and the second, *Lovelace Flats* by Reflex Press. She is currently working on a PhD on the role of (dis)connectivity in the novella-in-flash.

jupiter-jones@outlook.com @jupiterjonz

Dirty Boy

by James Hancock

Kyle Tomley was an awkward character and always had been. Not necessarily on any spectrum, or having any disability; just not quite right. His mum called him her special little soldier, yet he was as far from the makings of a soldier as you could get. Thin and frail, thick lens glasses due to his poor eyesight, an odd facial twitch, and a weak immune system. He averaged one cold every month. If there was a sneeze in the air, Kyle would catch it. He had a few friends and they were all comfortable to call themselves geeks or nerds. They liked games conventions, comic books, steam trains, and online computer gaming; being the social event of the week. Four nights a week to be precise. Kyle had just turned thirty years old, was still single, and was a failure when it came to the opposite sex. He'd only ever had one girlfriend; when he was nine. He didn't understand women and they didn't understand him.

Routine, organisation, and his job played a large part of Kyle's life, and when the local software company he worked for went bankrupt, his world was understandably destroyed. As always, he turned to his mum for advice.

'What can I do, Mum?'

She had advised to get another job quickly, but as Kyle couldn't drive it narrowed down the search considerably. He lived in an old and somewhat backward village, which meant finding a job that met his skills involved two buses and a train to get to a big town. He considered working for himself, online, and beefing up his gaming webpage, but that would take too long to get running. He needed to pay the bills now. So he looked for work locally. One job vacancy: Laundrette Manager. Yes, the village still had a laundrette. Kyle wasn't keen, but there was no other option. He made the call, got the interview, and asked the necessary questions... awkwardly.

The owner, Mrs Newman, had obviously liked him as Kyle got the job. How he managed it was beyond him, he'd mumbled nervously through the whole thing. But he got it. Likely he was the only person to apply. Unfortunately the job title had left out one important detail... Night Manager. Kyle couldn't fathom why his village needed a laundrette, let alone a twenty-four hour one, but apparently it did. The biggest problem and main thing on Kyle's mind was his online gaming night being cancelled. Well, the others would still play, but his level seventy paladin would get left behind for certain. Dammit!

Unsurprisingly, Kyle's first night on the eleven 'til seven shift was quiet, only one person all night. His friend Tony had popped along to say hello. Tony sat for thirty minutes and talked about a film that was being made; a film based on a game he had played and completed four times over the last ten years. The rest of the night would likely be spent staring at the room and thinking. Mostly thinking he wished he'd bought a book, or tablet, or his laptop so he could beef up his website. He hadn't thought it through properly. This was the ideal job whilst you planned and prepared for another job.

In the centre of the room were twelve large washing machines, back to back as two rows of six, and there were six big tumble dryers lining a wall facing them, twice as big as his tumble dryer at home. The other area of wall space was taken up with three fold-down ironing boards and a forty inch wall-mounted TV. The TV was the thing that would keep Kyle sane, but he was fully aware that if the machines were running there would be no chance of hearing it. Fortunately he had the graveyard shift, so noise was an unlikely problem. Unfortunately the batteries in the TV controller didn't work. He'd bring two AAA batteries with him tomorrow night and get the TV working. And speaking of sanity, Kyle remembered the last night manager... Jack or John Fullerton, if his memory served. He had been discretely taken off in a van one night, and not heard of again. Yes, it was in the local newspaper. Great! The hours were awful, the pay was barely minimum wage, and the prospects were, well, pretty bad. Kyle stared at the selection of kitchen chairs placed around the room... his choice of comfort for the night. Most were padded, but they had chunks gouged out. Who does that? Surely it doesn't happen by accident. Kyle felt depressed and wanted to quit, and probably would have, but he knew his mum would expect that. She'd expect him to last a few nights, have a meltdown and move back home. No! He was a big boy now, so he'd stick it out.

His mobile phone had 24% battery when he'd arrived, and after Tony had left and Kyle had given up rubbing the controller batteries in an attempt to give them some life, his phone was the sole sense of entertainment from 1am until 1:48am. And then it died. Tomorrow would be a better night. He'd be prepared. Now, what to do for the next five hours and twelve minutes?

Kyle was contemplating getting into a tumble dryer to see if he fitted inside. He knew he'd try it eventually, so why not get it out the way now.

And then he heard *The Voice*. 'Hey, big boy!'

Kyle checked his phone. No, that was dead. The TV was off, so not that. The door hadn't opened since Tony left over an hour ago. Where was it coming from?

'You're new here, right?' came the voice again.

There was someone hiding behind a washing machine. A woman. The voice was a woman's voice and it came from the washing machines. Kyle walked over to the machines, walked around them, and stood confused. There was nobody there.

'You're quite handsome,' said the voice. A woman's voice; probably about forty years old and with a sexy husky type of tone.

Kyle crouched and stared at the washing machine at the end of the line. The ones facing the TV. Was there a recording device in there or something? Had Tony planted something as a joke? No, he wasn't that kind of guy. As pranks go, this was too advanced for Tony. His idea of a joke would be to hide Kyle's lunch. Kyle looked at the chair with his backpack on and decided to check it and make sure his lunch was still there.

'My name's Martina,' said the washing machine.

Kyle fell backwards. Sitting on the floor, he stared at the washing machine for a few seconds. The voice had come from the washing machine, that was for certain, but... how? It must be some kind of joke. Yes, he was the new guy. He looked around the room for potential hidden cameras, imagining a group of people in a room laughing away at his expense.

'You're better looking than the last guy. Younger too,' Martina said.

Kyle couldn't see any cameras or devices that could be producing the voice, and the sound was too clear and real to be coming from anything like that. It was definitely coming from the washing machine; he was in no doubt about that. Not inside the drum, or from the soap drawer, but from it as a whole, as if it were a person talking, but without moving lips or a facial expression to go with the words being said.

Kyle felt like an idiot. 'Hello?'

'Oh good, you can hear me then,' Martina said, in a relieved tone. 'I was starting to worry.'

'Is this a joke?' asked Kyle.

'Is what a joke?' Martina asked.

'Err, you're talking to me. Is this a joke? Am I on TV or something?' Kyle smiled nervously.

'The TV hasn't been working for six days. It needs new batteries in the controller.' Martina's voice was confident and matter of fact.

There was an awkward pause. Kyle searched for a logical explanation, but there was none. This machine was definitely doing the talking. 'You're a washing machine,' Kyle said, unsure of what to say.

'Yes. And you're a human, male, I'd say mid twenties.' Martina's seductive tone was pleasant to hear, and Kyle felt a little flattered by her age guesstimate.

'Thirty. I'm thirty.' Kyle felt more awkward than normal. He didn't do well in social situations, and apparently it wasn't because of conversing with another human, apparently it covered communicating with, well, anything.

'And you look good for it.' Martina was flirting. Was she flirting?

'Thanks,' Kyle said. 'Err, how is this possible? I mean, you talking to me.' Kyle was still looking for a hidden device, but there was none. Martina was a talking washing machine. This was the factual truth.

Martina sighed, as if thinking on the question. 'How is anything possible? How are you able to talk, to make noise, to construct words through sound? How are the stars held up in the sky? What measures time, when did it begin, and when will it end? And if God made the universe then who or what made God?'

Kyle thought on Martina's words. 'I don't believe in God.'

'Then what made the universe?' she asked. 'There can't have been something which suddenly just sparked and came to life from nothing, right? So if no God, the universe must have simply always been there. Try and get your head around that.' Martina certainly made some thought-provoking points.

'I guess,' said Kyle.

'Well, in answer to your question, that's how. It's the great unexplained.' Martina's voice was calming. Pleasant.

'Anything is possible.' Kyle couldn't believe he was having an in-depth conversation with a washing machine. Not just any old washing machine too, but one he'd just met.

'Even the impossible is often proved possible,' Martina added.

Kyle nodded his agreement.

'Now, the TV doesn't work, so we're in for a long night,' Martina said. 'Do you have any tricks or stories you can tell to keep me amused?'

Kyle wasn't the 'party tricks' kind of guy, and his stories were the things that usually spurred women to find an excuse to leave. No, he wasn't going to mess this up, Martina seemed nice and although she was just a washing machine, she was clearly a female washing machine, and Kyle was holding a pretty good conversation so far. 'I-Spy?' he asked.

'Okay,' said Martina in a surprisingly enthusiastic manner. 'But be warned, I'm very good at this.'

Kyle's competitive side was concerned. She obviously had a limited visual range, and who knows how long she had stared at and examined the same area before her. She would know every little nook and cranny. I-Spy might have been a big mistake.

'I'll go first,' Kyle said.

The next night, Kyle had come prepared. Batteries, laptop, phone charger, a chess set, and his favourite board game... Risk. After his thrashing at I-Spy last night, Kyle was reclaiming some masculinity, and what better way of showing how manly you are than invading and holding Asia? Five access points, difficult to conquer, but worth seven extra armies. Tonight was a night to impress.

It wasn't surprising that Martina was where Kyle had left her... last on the row of six. She was the cleanest and best looking of the washing machines on the row. Actually, the best looking of all twelve washing machines in the room. Kyle had worn jeans and a t-shirt yesterday, and Martina was all over his looks and how young and smart he was. Tonight he had upped his game; cream Chinos and a chocolate brown shirt. He was dressing to impress. And impressed she was. Within the first five minutes of Kyle's arrival, Martina had complimented his clothes, hair, and his strength at being able to carry a laptop and a board game at the same time. Kyle played it cool. It was nothing.

Tony came by at eleven thirty again, and Kyle got rid of him as quickly as possible. This was going to be an epic night. A night to impress. And Martina was. So impressed in fact that when Kyle played three cavalry cards, deployed his troops in southern Europe and took Africa in one turn, Martina made a low sighing noise that sounded quite sexual. She couldn't help herself, and even though her dice roll, which Kyle had rolled for her, was better than his, she was a victim of his superior tactics. He had totally schooled her at the game and in less than three hours she was out and he was victorious.

'You were very forceful then,' Martina said, in her sultry tone.

Kyle played it cool; nothing needed to be said. He carried on packing up the game.

'You knew what you wanted and you took it,' said Martina. 'I like that in a man.'

Kyle raised an eyebrow and nodded in the best James Bond way he could muster. He opened a bottle of fizzy orange Lucozade and took a manly gulp.

'It made me wet,' said Martina.

Lucozade spurted and frothed out from Kyle's nostrils and he began to choke.

'Are you okay?' Martina sounded both sexy and concerned.

'Yep,' wheezed Kyle. He coughed a few times and wiped the orange from his top lip with the cuff of his shirt. 'Chess?' he asked in a squeaky tone.

'Oh yes,' said Martina in a way that didn't fit the question. A way that made Kyle wonder if she knew what chess was. Kyle might have won at Risk, but Martina was dominating the seduction. Kyle took a moment whilst he set up the chessboard, a moment to think about what was happening here. Was he on a date? This was too weird. Martina was a washing machine. A very sexual and seductive washing machine. She was in control, experienced, and with a hint of Italian in her sultry voice. Well, she was an Indesit.

It was a good game and Kyle was victorious once again.

When he played chess with Tony, Kyle played it to win, but it was different with Martina, he found himself purposefully losing some unneeded pieces just so he could hear her say, 'I take your pawn.'

'We should play again. But this time spice it up a bit,' Martina said.

'What did you have in mind?' Kyle was aware that he was now speaking in a slightly lower and more seductive tone himself. He was one step away from going full Clint Eastwood. He'd need to rein it in a little.

'When I take a pawn, you undo a button,' Martina said. 'And if I take your bishop, you remove your trousers.'

Kyle nearly mentioned that there were two bishops and only one pair of trousers, but he stopped himself, realising that the bishop she referenced and the way she referenced it might have been more suggestive and less about actual game rules. Either way, Kyle found himself agreeing. And what unfolded went down in Kyle's mental history book as one of the strangest yet most erotic things he had ever done. Chess was no longer a game for old Russian men with beards.

Kyle sat opposite Martina, in his pants, and realised that she had learned a great deal from that first game. Had he been hustled?

'Now, open my door and put your clothes inside,' Martina said in a commanding manner. Kyle did as he was told.

'Now touch my drawer,' she added.

Kyle touched Martina's soap drawer. He tried to make it sexy and used the back of his hand.

'Slowly,' she said.

Kyle slowed it down a little and Martina made some noises of appreciation. Kyle pouted his lips and closed his eyes as Martina's moans intensified.

'Open it,' she whispered.

Kyle opened her soap drawer. She sighed and moaned. Kyle stroked his hand over the glass door and up the side of the metal casing. Martina liked that a lot.

'Turn me on,' Martina gasped.

Kyle looked a little confused, unsure what it was he had been doing, but then realised that she meant it in the literal sense. 'I haven't got any soap powder.'

'Are you dirty? Are you a dirty boy?' Martina asked.

'Yes. Very,' said Kyle. He pushed his face against the soap drawer and started to blow gently. The laundrette door opened and a fat man carrying two bin bags full of clothes walked in.

Kyle panicked and scurried on all fours away from Martina and towards the other end of the washing machines. As the fat man moved, so did Kyle, keeping low and on all fours, he shuffled as quietly as possible to the other side and out of the fat man's sight. The fat man stood looking down at a laptop, board game, and Kyle's other belongings. There was no explaining his way out of this. There was no way of getting out of here unseen either. Kyle tapped into his newly found confidence and stood up. He walked around the washing machines and to his things, smiling at the fat man and giving him the typical greeting nod. The fat man stared back in disbelief.

'This one's out of order,' said Kyle, opened Martina's door, took out his clothes and started to get dressed.

The fat man slid his bags across the laundrette floor and to the washing machine at the other end. He loaded his clothes inside whilst glancing over at Kyle. Kyle finished getting dressed, picked up his things, and walked out.

Kyle waited across the street in between the fish and chip shop and a collection of large bins, crouched low, uncomfortable, and staring at the laundrette. His laundrette. The fat man didn't leave for over two hours, and Kyle's shift was nearly over. When the coast was clear, Kyle hurried back to the laundrette, flipped the *Open* sign to *Closed*, locked the door and rushed over to Martina.

'I'm so sorry,' said Kyle, crouching down to Martina's level.

'You scared me. You just left and I didn't know where you were.' Martina sounded upset.

'I know. I'm sorry.' Kyle rubbed his hands over his face. 'Did he use you?'

'No. He used the two on the end,' Martina said, some calm returning to her voice.

The thought of someone else using Martina upset Kyle. A strange feeling of anger came over him. 'It won't happen again. I promise,' Kyle said confidently.

'Do you? Do you promise me, Kyle?' Martina asked.

Kyle put his hand on his heart. 'Yes. I promise.'

Kyle couldn't sleep. His mind ran wild with images of men dumping their load in Martina, forcefully and without a care. Kicking her if she misbehaved. He got up, got dressed, and headed out with purpose. He needed to see Martina; even if it was Mrs Henderson's shift. He needed to see Martina now!

Kyle arrived at the laundrette in the late morning. The room was alive with people, feeding clothes from bags into machines, pulling them from dryers into baskets, and... who was that man? A good-looking man had just finished putting soap powder into Martina's drawer and had slammed it shut with unnecessary force. Where was Mrs Henderson? There she was, the fat cow, sat on a chair and reading a book. Had she not seen the man? It was her job to keep watch and to protect the machines from such ruffians. Kyle stared at the man through the window, stared through gritted teeth, his eyes widening as the man treated Martina the way he did. The man, tanned skin, probably foreign. Kyle wasn't racist, but he was finding things he disliked about him, his looks, and the fact that he shouldn't be in the laundrette. He probably shouldn't be in the country. What was going on? Kyle never thought that way. Right! If Mrs Henderson wasn't going to do anything about it, Kyle would. He forcefully rapped his knuckles against the window.

The man looked around at Kyle. Kyle waved a finger, pointed at Martina and mouthed the word, 'NO!'

The good-looking foreign man frowned, confused, and looked about to see if it was indeed himself who was being glared at by the strange man at the window... the angry man whose face was red with rage.

Kyle put two fingers to his eyes and then pointed at the man... *I'm watching you!* And with that Kyle stormed off.

Something needed to be done, something to protect and keep the laundrette safe. Kyle was the night manager, and if the morning manager couldn't cope, Kyle would have to step up and take charge.

Kyle wasn't taking any chances, and as his shift started that night he locked the laundrette door and turned the sign to read *Closed*. Hardly anyone came in anyway, and he didn't want another awkward and embarrassing episode like last night.

'I hate daytime.' Martina's first words as Kyle sat in front of her.

'Something bad happen?' Kyle asked. He already knew the answer. He knew the way she was treated in the day.

'No. It's just the wait. It's too long before we can be together again,' Martina said.

'I know what you mean,' said Kyle. 'Anyway, we are alone now, and I have locked the door so we can be together uninterrupted.'

There was a silence. 'Are you okay?' Kyle asked.

Martina sniffed as if she was near to crying. 'I know it has only been a few nights, but I... I think I love you, Kyle.'

Kyle paused. He could sense Martina's emotions. They washed over him and filled him up inside. 'I love you too.'

'I want to play with you, Kyle,' Martina said, in a slow and sexual manner.

Kyle smiled. He knew what she meant. Oh yes! He slid his hand into the backpack he'd brought with him and produced the chess set. 'Chess?'

'You read my mind you naughty boy.' Martina's voice practically purred.

Kyle set up the board quicker than ever. 'I'll go first.' Kyle's words were confident, just how Martina liked it. Martina had unleashed his inner man.

'Ooh,' sighed Martina, as Kyle slid a pawn slowly forward across the chessboard, gazing at her longingly the whole time.

Things happened that night. Strange things that Kyle hadn't experienced before. Good things. Naughty things. And it's true what they say about women getting in the way of friendships; Kyle hadn't even noticed Tony when he came by at eleven thirty. And fortunately, Tony hadn't noticed Kyle either.

Martina's voice was quiet, no more than a whisper. 'Wake up, lover boy.'

Kyle opened his eyes. He ached all over. He must have fallen asleep in front of Martina, on the cold hard floor. It was daytime, bright, sunny, and there was a knocking on the door.

'Someone's here,' whispered Martina.

Kyle looked up to see an old lady with a shopping trolley looking at him through the glass of the laundrette door, squinting as she tried to take in what she was looking at. Kyle was naked.

Kyle cupped his manhood in his hands and ran over to the door. He nodded at the sign. 'We're closed!'

The old lady didn't look at the sign, she had a close-up view now and was trying to get a better look at Kyle in all his glory. 'What?' she asked.

'Fuck off!' Kyle snapped, removed a hand and waved for the old lady to go away.

And then Kyle saw her... Mrs Henderson, the morning manager, crossing the street to begin her shift. She had a key. Kyle had to act quickly. What to do? He grabbed hold of the nearest tumble dryer and started to move it towards the door. Well, he attempted to, it was a beast of a machine and only budged slightly. Kyle groaned out loud and then relaxed his grip, defeated.

'You'll get arrested, you know,' said the old lady from the other side of the door. Kyle was in a panic and the old lady was an unwelcome annoyance. He gave her the middle finger and the old lady gasped with shock. Shock, or due to Kyle being in full display. He was past wasting time trying to cover up.

'You can do it, Kyle.' Martina's voice giving Kyle the boost he needed. Determined and fuelled by Martina's love, he grabbed the tumble dryer again and roared out loud as he pulled it away from the wall and towards the door. Mrs Henderson arrived beside the old lady as Kyle shimmied the tumble dryer from its corner to corner, walking it the short distance to the door. Initially slowed by what she was looking at, Mrs Henderson snapped out of it and quickly fumbled for her keys, but it was too late. Kyle pushed the tumble dryer up against the glass door and collapsed.

'My hero,' said Martina.

'Open the door, Mr. Tomley.' Mrs Henderson glared at Kyle.

'We're closed,' was all that Kyle could muster. Out of

breath he slowly sat up. 'Go away, Mrs Henderson. You're not needed today.'

Mrs Henderson reached into her handbag and took out her mobile phone. Kyle stood up and walked back to Martina.

'Will you get in trouble?' Martina asked.

Kyle shook his head. 'No. And I'm not leaving you. I promised I'd stay, and they can't make me go.' Kyle placed a hand on top of Martina.

'You make me so happy, Kyle,' said Martina.

'I've phoned the police,' said Mrs Henderson from the laundrette door.

The situation was difficult and Kyle wasn't certain how things would pan out, but at least he had found the time to get dressed and make himself more presentable when PC Wilton and PC Allan arrived. He rested a hand on top of Martina, closed his eyes, and sighed.

'Wish me luck, baby,' he whispered. He had gone full Clint Eastwood.

'Good luck,' said Martina, softly.

Kyle walked over to the laundrette door. There was now a collection of six passers-by stood with the two policemen, the old lady, and Mrs Henderson. The old Kyle would have felt intimidated by ten people staring at him, and some of them with expressions of anger, but the new Kyle was confident. Martina's love gave him the necessary self-belief. He was the one in charge here.

'Can you open the door please, sir?' PC Wilton was a big

man, and the obvious negotiator. PC Allan mumbled something on his walkie-talkie.

'You'll need to talk with the owner, my boss,' said Kyle. 'I'm doing the day shift today. She'll understand.'

'I need you to open the door please, sir,' repeated PC Wilton.

'Didn't he hear you?' asked Martina.

'Didn't you hear me?' asked Kyle.

'Yes, sir. We've already spoken with your boss, and I am asking you for the last time to open the door.' PC Wilton looked around at PC Allan, who gave him a nod.

'No, I'm not going anywhere until I see Mrs Newman. She's the owner, not you. She'll understand.' Kyle made sure his tone was forceful and wouldn't be questioned. He wasn't about giving off the wrong impression.

'Well said.' Martina's voice came from the middle of the room. 'If they want to force you out, they'll need to call in the fire brigade and blast you out.'

Kyle was in charge here. This was his laundrette and he wasn't going to get bossed about by outsiders. 'Either get Mrs Newman, or call in the fire brigade to bash the door down, but I'm not opening it until I speak to her,' Kyle said.

Mrs Henderson passed the door key to PC Wilton, who unlocked it and tried to force it open, but the tumble dryer held it in place.

'If you try to come in, I'll get all the machine's going and foam the place out.' Kyle looked nervous. 'I have suds!' Kyle added.

'That won't be necessary, sir,' said PC Wilton.

Kyle backed off to Martina. 'I don't think it's working. What can I do?'

'Fight for me, baby. Fight for your love,' Martina said. Kyle nodded and gritted his teeth ready, psyching himself up for the inevitable battle.

PC Wilton produced his police baton and extended it ready.

Kyle closed his eyes and placed a hand on top of Martina. 'I love you. Remember that. No matter what happens, I love you.'

PC Wilton smashed out the window with his baton and started to climb through the door.

'Die for me my darling,' whispered Martina.

PC Wilton was inside the laundrette and it would only be a matter of time before the cuffs were on. Kyle wasn't going down without a fight. Some things were worth fighting for, and this was one of them. The laundrette was his chessboard, and he was the king.

Martina's voice echoed in Kyle's ears. 'Die for me.' He let out a mighty roar and charged across the room at PC Wilton.

PC Allan's taser found its mark, Kyle made a noise that was part squeal and part whimper, and then collapsed. He twitched and moaned through gritted teeth, a wet patch forming around the crotch of his cream Chinos. PC Wilton leaned over Kyle and slapped on the handcuffs. Checkmate.

Three days later, an advertisement was placed on the notice board of the village supermarket. *Laundrette Manager Required*. Manager... the term excited Harry Pullman, fresh out of college, and out to impress. Like so many young men, he wasn't blessed with good looks or confidence, so this could be the exact thing he needed. He jotted down the phone number. If being a manager of somewhere didn't attract the ladies, what would?

James Hancock is a writer/screenwriter of comedy, thriller, horror, sci-fi and twisted fairy tales. A few of his short screenplays have been made into films, and he has been published in print magazines, online, and in anthology books.

He lives in England, with his wife and two daughters. And a bunch of pets he insisted his girls could NOT have.

The Librarian

by Sam Derby

Behind the broad wooden counter stood the librarian. She was tuned into the silence. Her feet were encased in soft plimsolls, and they did not scuff the polished floorboards over which she glided, between the reserve shelves and the counter and the trolley. She stood poised, as if ready to jump. Or perhaps she was just listening to a particular disturbance in the air - someone at the back of the rare books room had torn a leaf, a shelf ticket had fluttered to the floor, the colonel was muttering in his sleep again.

She was not the head librarian. The head librarian was less nimble, not so tuned in anymore to the silence. She bided her time: the kick-step needed mending, the books were heavy, and the shelves were high. That was a rare dark thought; most days, she bided her time peacefully and with due regard for process. She listened to the silence, and did her job. She could tell what each reader wanted; she knew where the best books were kept.

'Excuse me,' said a young man. He was wearing a stained tweed jacket over port-wine trousers. She had listened to him turning pages: a quarto, eighteenth century, decent paper. He had turned them with increasing ferocity, back and forth, chapters at a time, whole sections falling onto the table. He had ordered the wrong book.

'I think I've - are you sure this is the right book?'

She took it in her tough, slim fingers and opened it like a jewel box. It was the book he had ordered: the identical shelf-mark was on the slip inside the cover. It was not one of the best books. She imagined the stacks fifty feet below the pavement, letting her mind drift along the dark corridors, each ceiling-light in turn flickering on with some reluctance ahead of her. She imagined the heavily-geared wheel turning to move the stacks apart. In the new space thus created, she visualised the books on the bottom shelf, one by one, from left to right.

'You meant to order the first edition,' she said, simply, beginning to fill in the order slip.

'I don't think so - I mean, I spoke to the head librarian,' said the young man, at which she prevented herself from looking up at him, 'and she said...'

'The first edition is the book that you want,' she said, still looking at the order slip, 'with the argument, in verse, between the preface and the address to the reader.'

'Yes,' he said, as she looked him squarely in the eye, so that he blushed very slightly. 'That's right, thank you,' he said, slightly more loudly than necessary.

A woman with ironed-flat hair looked up for a beat, and then looked down; a whispered conversation by the stairwell was interrupted; the colonel almost woke.

She moved silently away, pushed the slip into the vacuum tube, and returned to her post. The young man paused at the counter. He had blue eyes.

'I wouldn't bother, actually,' she said, looking up at him again, 'you'll find our copy is just a fragment.'

'A fragment?'

'Just the frontispiece, and the envoi. Nothing else, not even a catch-word.'

'I see,' he said.

'The Duke of Albemarle's library has a mint copy.'

'Ah,' he said, the soft light of hope illuminating his face, which seemed quite pleasant, now that she looked at it.

'I can see if we might borrow it for you.'

'Would you?' She nodded, moving out from behind the counter, towards an old man almost lost within the pages of an immense folio. It, in turn, sat deep in a pile of foam book-rests within the shadows of which the heads and tails of book-snakes could occasionally be glimpsed.

'Your Grace,' she said, in his ear, 'someone's asking for the book again.'

The Duke sat up slowly, and pushed his half-moon glasses back up his nose. 'It's out of the question,' he said, with great clarity, before resuming his studies.

'I'm very sorry,' she said.

'Are there any other copies? I feel sure that you must know,' said the young man, looking back at her. He had tidied his hair somewhat while she had been talking to the Duke. He had cleaned his glasses, too.

'There are none,' she said. 'And - is there any way, do you think, if perhaps at a different time you were to ask...'

She had been there, to the Duke's great, dilapidated Hall, surrounded by decaying farmland. The library was in great danger from the creeping damp, and she had catalogued its books for him one Christmas, her thin frame shivering despite jumpers and scarves piled upon one another, despite the decent fire raised by the Duke's one remaining servant. The book was in a cabinet behind a glass door, between a First Folio and a bound set of civil war newspapers. The door to the Hall was never locked; the door to the library was off its hinges; the cabinet was flimsy and could be picked at will. She had thought all of this before, in idleness, mostly. Now she looked back at the young man, with his unadorned ring finger to match hers, with his crumpled trousers and his hesitant smile.

She looked around the library, at the sleeping colonel and the woman with the ironed-flat hair. She thought of the dark cool corridors beneath the earth where the good books were, where she could tread softly and summon the light as she moved. She thought of the head librarian, and the sixty-fourth birthday card standing on the mantelpiece in her office.

She looked back at the young man, and said, 'it's out of the question.'

He paused for a moment, and then turned and walked away. As he did so, out of the corner of her eye, she caught sight of the head librarian, shuffling ominously towards the high shelves at the back of the room. With no hesitation, and yet a sharp pang of loss, she said, 'Watch out for that kick-step.'

Sam Derby is an Oxford, UK based writer of short stories. Credits include: Long-listed, Bath Short Story Award 2019; 3rd, ChipLitFest Short Story Competition (judged by Nicholas Royle) and HC Manchester Fiction Prize Short Story 2019. Published by Ghosts & Scholars, Storgy, Coffin Bell, Schlock, The Quiet Reader, Horla. His work has also been published in several anthologies by the Oxford Writing Circle of which he is a member.

www.samderby1975.wordpress.com
@samderby9
Instagram: samderby75

The One About The Sheep

by Sally Bramley

At heart, Reuben Jacks is not a sheep rustler. Yet, here he is, on a sunny afternoon in July, driving back across the Brecon Beacons, heading for home, with someone else's sheep curled up in the back of his work van.

He follows the single-track road as it threads its way across the hills. The grass in the middle of the road swishes against the bottom of his van. It bounces over the ruts and he leaves his seat.

'Bloody hell,' he says.

His sleeves are rolled up and the windows are open wide. He can see the hairs on his arms ruffling like corn moving in the breeze. He feels the tickling on his skin. He leans forward, holding the wheel with one hand and peels his damp shirt away from his back.

If he tilts the mirror, he can see the animal sleeping, a mass of sheep's wool on a hessian sack by the wheel arch. He can smell it too, a warm mix of greasiness and muck. He's had little to do with sheep. He doesn't dislike them, exactly. He certainly loves the smell of roast lamb. The woody tang of rosemary. The smooth mint sauce. It's one of Jeannie's specialities; a signature dish she calls it, although she hasn't cooked it much of late. But that is more his kind of thing. Not live sheep.

It was Mrs Davy's fault that he was there at all, saying that since she'd moved house, she couldn't find a gardener in the whole of Wales, not one as reliable as him, anyway. How likely was that? She'd asked him to come and sort out her new garden.

'I just can't do the heavy work myself.' Her voice wavered over the phone. 'Naturally, I'll pay for your bed and breakfast in the village.'

'I'm not one for travelling,' Reuben said.

'It's only Wales.' She clicked her tongue against her teeth and it rattled in his ear. 'Just over the bridge. A passport will not be required.'

He felt his face redden, even though she couldn't see him. He ran one hand forwards over his scalp against the short stubble. And he wondered whether being away from Jeannie for a while might not be a bad idea.

'Just for a week, mind,' he said, eventually, as if he was struggling to fit her into his busy schedule.

Mrs Davy may have been responsible for his visit to Wales, but the sheep element of this adventure was definitely down to Albert. On the Tuesday before the trip, he and Reuben met up in the Bristol Flyer. This was normal for a Tuesday evening; being in the pub was nothing to do with the arguments with Jeannie. Reuben was sharing his lack of travel experience.

'What do you mean you've never been over the bridge?' Albert said. He sat back grasping his glass in one hand, forgetting to drink for a moment. 'How can you not have been over the bridge?'

Reuben shrugged. 'Had no reason to.'

Albert's eyebrows lifted and he shook his head. After a second pint, he decided to share his knowledge of Wales. He sat back, his small eyes wrinkled up, as if he could see it in the distance.

'So,' he said. 'It's full of sheep, for a start.' He waved his arm through the air indicating their presence. 'Sheep everywhere. All over the mountains. Bleating and shitting and carrying on.' Albert knew everything about animals, so he said, because he owned a butcher's shop.

'Right.' Reuben lifted his glass and emptied it into his mouth. The beer warmed his insides as it went down.

He returned from the bar carrying two more pints and, before he could sit down, Albert was leaning across the table and jabbing a finger at him. 'I tell you what,' he said. 'I've got a crackin' idea.'

'Uhuh.' Reuben had come across a few of Albert's ideas in his time. He sat down.

'You should bring one back. A sheep. I'll get it dispatched and we'll split it between us. It'll fill both our freezers, no problem.'

Reuben swallowed and wiped his mouth with the back of his hand. 'I can't just buy a sheep!' he said. 'Would a farmer even sell me one?'

Albert sniggered. 'You don't need to buy one. They

wander about on the mountains. If you come back over the tops there'll be sheep everywhere just for the taking.'

Reuben rubbed his hand around the back of his neck. 'I think you get transported for doing things like that.'

Albert breathed out with a noise. 'Don't be daft. Those days have long gone. Anyway ...they don't belong to anyone. They're wild. Like rabbits.'

Reuben shook his head. 'Someone must have put them there.'

But nevertheless, after another two pints and Albert's reminders about the smell of roast lamb, Reuben found himself persuaded. Of course, sheep didn't belong to anyone. They were free to roam. And who was going to miss an odd sheep, anyway? They wouldn't actually count them, surely?

Reuben told Jeannie that he would be working in North Wales during the following week. They were sitting in the kitchen eating supper. He concentrated on his chicken and chips and didn't look up as he spoke. He could hear his own voice, higher than usual, tight in his throat. But it wasn't such a big deal, was it?

He knew that it was.

'What do you mean?' Jeannie said. Her fork was in mid-air between plate and mouth.

'Mrs Davy asked me and I couldn't say no. You know what she's like.'

'But do you have to go now? I thought... There are things we need to talk about.'

Reuben chewed slowly. At last he said, 'It's only for a week.'

Jeannie put her fork down and gave up on her supper. She had that creased, pale look that had become familiar to him. That made him hurt inside as if his muscles were in spasm.

When she spoke again, she said quietly. 'I guess a few days away will give us both some time to think.'

He breathed in quickly, suddenly afraid that they had crossed a line. 'I'll be back on Friday,' he said.

It was quiet. He could hear the clock ticking. The traffic some distance away. Jeannie nodded but didn't meet his eyes. And he wished he could be someone else for her. Someone who felt differently.

He tried to make her smile then and told her about Albert and what he'd said about Wales. And about the sheep plan.

'Albert's an idiot,' she said with her back to him moving the heaped plates onto the side.

'That's just what I thought,' he said, breathing out with a croak of a laugh. 'I won't be doing any sheep stealing in a hurry.'

But Jeannie missed the laugh and the words. She'd already left the room.

Reuben stayed on at the table, sitting back, staring at the door, wondering how things had ended up like this. Three years they had been together now, yet he couldn't remember them ever disagreeing so strongly about something.

When they'd married, he could remember feeling...so many feelings. Shock. Relief. Happiness, maybe. He'd certainly felt surprised to find that he might have a normal life like other people. Even at his age it was possible. In fact, neither of them were teenagers. He was just amazed to meet a woman who wanted to know him. Someone who seemed to notice who he was.

Grateful. Most of all he felt grateful.

The weather was kind to Reuben and he spent the week digging flower beds, repairing garden walls. Feeling the soil between his fingers and under his nails. Feeling the familiar aches in his body that soothed him and reminded him of who he was.

And there were conversations going on in his head every day – with Jeannie, with himself. With some other being, God maybe. But as he bent and stretched and reached to the highest branches, or pushed his foot down on the spade, loosening the compacted earth, these movements made his thinking easier. It was as though the thoughts already existed in his mind and were simply moved along by his actions. And that made his shoulders relax and his breath deepen for a while.

In amongst all his thinking, he thought most of all about Jeannie.

Jeannie was a librarian. Is a librarian. She has been a librarian all her life so she knows things. She reads lots of books. Like a lot of books. He likes that about her, although he worries that she knows so much more than him about everything. He assumes that she can see straight through him. But he likes that she reads so much. It suits him that he doesn't have to speak all the time because he isn't one for constant chatting.

Sometimes he sits and watches her as she reads, carefully peering around his newspaper so that she won't notice. She stares at the page, turning it quickly when she needs to. Even anticipating that point and holding the page between her fingers, ready, not wanting to waste a moment.

As she stares at the words, her face flickers and changes. He can see her feelings race across her skin like clouds in front of the sun, shadows skimming over the earth. A smile. Or deep furrows between her eyes. Her teeth chewing at her bottom lip. Once he caught sight of a small pool gathering at the bottom of one eye and he waited, holding his breath, for it to become a proper tear and spill down her face. But just before it was about to fall, she wiped it away with the side of her hand. And he breathed out again, quietly relieved for her.

At times, he tries to guess what she might be reading that creates these feelings. Occasionally, her mouth will fall open and a sound might escape. A small 'Oh'. And then she will look up, suddenly, her face pink as she wonders if she has been observed. When this happens, he quickly looks back at his paper and pretends nothing is happening. Nothing has been noticed. And she will sigh and return to her book.

It was at one of these times that Reuben finally realised that he loves her.

This reading of hers, this way she has of concentrating so hard on someone else's words. It aches and warms his bones in ways that he has never imagined. And he wonders if he has ever inspired such feelings in her. He is pretty sure that wouldn't have happened.

By the end of the week the garden was neat and tidy, the grass cut, the edges clipped, manure on the roses. A couple of tubs on the patio to give some colour. He stood back to look at it, breathing out with a satisfied noise. Then he took his leave and his pay packet from Mrs Davy and headed for home.

At midday, he pulled into a passing place high up in the mountains. He wiped the sweat from his face with his sleeve. He opened all the van doors to get a breeze blowing through and then sat in his seat, his legs out of the door, and ate his packed lunch.

He was at the top of a long shallow valley dotted with sheep munching at the scrubby grass. 'Sheep everywhere,' Albert had said and he was right about that. The lambs were almost fully grown now with thick wool on their bodies and bare faces. Neat and tidy. But the mothers were something else. Dirty wool falling away in long threads as if they had already lost half of it in a fight. Spindly legs. Scraggy, untidy bodies. Muck around their rear ends. They certainly didn't look very appetising. They bleated now and then for no apparent reason.

They all ignored him, concentrating on their chewing, heads down, wandering close.

Eventually, Reuben got out of the van and stretched his arms, reaching up to the sky as he breathed. He leaned on the van roof and looked out over the mountains, the heat from the metal warming his chest. He sighed. He wasn't in any great hurry to get home.

The gorse was starting to yellow. Rank smells came from it on the breeze. Way out, as far as he could see, there were more hills that disappeared in the haze, and a river, white in the sunshine. The only sounds – apart from the sheep - were the birds, skylarks, he thought, twittering high over his head.

Jeannie would love this. That's what came into his mind. He could picture her face relaxing as she looked at the view. She would breathe out with a satisfied sigh. He would have liked to bring her here, to this place, and hear that sigh.

Now, he wondered if that would ever happen. His eyes were suddenly damp and his face felt a wobble coming on. He pulled his handkerchief from his pocket and blew his nose. He wasn't sure if they would ever get over this. He hadn't rung her all week, even though his missing of her was like a wound in his ribs. He didn't know what to say.

And he wondered what she would have been doing while he was gone. He tried to picture her at work, taking books from customers, carefully opening the first page and wielding a stamp to mark them with the date.

'We don't do that anymore,' she had told him once. Smiling.

'I think I'm pregnant,' Jeannie had said one morning in that straightforward way of hers. He could see she was trying hard not to grin. But her face beamed, her skin pink, her eyes wet. And he couldn't stop smiling either. When he was working, or in the pub, or eating his supper across the table from Jeannie, he would suddenly realise that his face was grinning. It made him think of Jeannie's reading.

It was like that for two months.

But it hadn't worked out as they had hoped.

As Reuben stood looking out over the mountains, images flitted through his mind. The worried expression on Jeannie's face when she told him she was bleeding. The drive to the hospital with her skin as white as the first snowdrops. People dashing everywhere. The noise and speed of everything. And then later, the quiet. The silence. The slow drive home. Jeannie's face. These are the things he still sees when he closes his eyes.

But now. Now she wants to try again. Try? He thought they'd both tried their best the first time. What else were they meant to do?

Time to get going. He couldn't stay away forever. He went around to the back of the van to shut the doors. As he did this, one of the sheep, wandered up to him on its skinny legs, its knees dirty, as if it had been kneeling in the mud. Maybe a youngish one but it looked fully grown. Suddenly it turned away from him, peered into his van and then bent its legs slightly. Before he realised what it was doing, it leapt straight into the back. It turned around, circled until it was happy and then knelt down and settled on the pile of hessian sacks.

'Well, I never,' Reuben said. 'Out! Come on, out. You're not going anywhere.'

The sheep peered up at him its ears sticking up like bats ears, pink on the inside. Its face was smooth. Black marks around its mouth and nose and underneath its eyes made him think of miners emerging from twelve hours down the pit. Thick wool surrounded its head like a polo-necked sweater. Its jaw moved rhythmically, chewing the insides of its mouth.

'For God's sake! How stupid must you be?' he said. His voice rose as the sheep ignored him. 'Get out!'

Reuben looked around for help. He didn't like to grab the sheep in case it bit him. Did sheep bite? He had no idea. But there was no-one around to come to his rescue; just mountains and sheep. He stood for a minute or two waiting for something to happen but nothing did. The larks kept on twittering. The other sheep wandered and bleated.

Finally, he slammed the doors shut, climbed back into the driver's seat and headed off, muttering to himself. Driving south, back towards his home.

So. Here he is. Here he is with a sheep in the back of his van, looking very much like a sheep rustler. Angry with the sheep for getting itself rustled. For taking the liberty of jumping into his van.

'Be it on your own head,' he says to it over his shoulder. 'You shouldn't have got in my van without asking.' He does know how stupid that sounds.

Then he drives back towards the bridge and his home. And he forgets all about the sheep.

As the sun starts to sink and Reuben pulls down the visor, he feels something tickling the side of his face. He jumps and the van swerves, hitting the grass verge and skidding back again. The road is empty but he feels a wave of heat pass over his body.

'Strewth!' he says. He turns, thinking there must be a

spider or something, dangling, but it is the sheep. It is standing behind him facing forwards peering over his shoulder.

He raises his elbow and pushes its head away. 'Lie down,' he says in a deep voice as if it is a dog needing a firm hand.

The sheep moves away slightly, although it carries on standing behind him.

'Jesus,' Reuben says. 'Bloody sheep.' As if he knows all about sheep. As if he carries them in his van every day.

As he comes down off the mountains, he feels something on his face again. This time it isn't so unexpected. He feels a weight on his shoulder. Something on his cheek. He glances sideways. The sheep has its head resting on his left shoulder, its right ear tickling the side of his face. It is staring straight ahead as if keen to see where it is going. It looks so serious, its black and white face pointing forwards, as though at any minute it is going to give him directions. At the third exit... a laugh rumbles in Reuben's throat and the noise surprises him. How long is it since he's laughed?

The sheep stays there for the next hour, feeling heavier as it relaxes, the warmth of its head spreading through Reuben's neck and shoulder. It moves with him as he rounds bends, leaning, swaying slightly. Grinding its teeth now and then, a quiet rumble in his ear. It breathes out regularly with a little 'humph' noise. The wool, soft and warm leaning against Reuben's body is comforting. One of Albert's crude jokes about lonely men and sheep comes to mind and, for a while, Reuben pushes the sheep away from him. But it soon returns and he lets it be.

As they near the Severn Bridge, Reuben pulls off the road into a lay-by, opens the driver's door and sits looking out across the river. What is he going to do? He thinks about his life. About how he imagined it would be. He lets himself think about how it would have been to be a parent. He knows he would have tried so hard to be a good father, even though he hasn't much experience of such things, so he isn't sure that he would know how. But he would have tried. He would have tried really hard to learn how. He would even have read books. Like loads of books.

And he looks across the river to the city that is his home and sits listening to the birds and the distant traffic.

'The thing is...' he says, finally, into the quiet. He looks around to make sure no-one is listening. 'The thing is, Sheep, it's been hard.' And he tells the sheep everything. Right from the beginning. He tells it about Jeannie, the unexpectedness of her appearing in his life. About how much he wanted to be a father. 'I never imagined my life could be like that,' he says. 'And then suddenly it seemed possible. We could have been a family. One of those proper happy families.' His voice cracks and breaks and the words disappear and he sits in silence for a while. The sheep continues to stare and chew and breathe.

'But it didn't happen,' he says. And he tells the sheep what had happened, as if it needed to know every detail. The responsibility he had felt. How hurt Jeannie had been. How he had to be strong for her. The way his body had shaken and trembled when he was alone. He had felt as if his bones could no longer hold him up. As though, the disappointment would burst out of him. That huge disappointment.

As well as the fear, of course. He even tells the sheep about that. That he is scared it was his fault in some way.

He is surprised to find that he knows the words. That once he starts it is possible to say them. That he is able to talk about all these things. He'd thought that he couldn't do that. He feels tears slipping down his cheeks and off his chin. 'I couldn't bear it,' he says and his voice gurgles and the tears keep coming.

'But you see, Sheep,' he says at last, mumbling through his handkerchief. 'Now she says she wants to try again.'

Reuben is quiet for a long while. He listens to the sheep chewing and breathing. The birds in the hedgerow by the van. The distant traffic heading for the bridge.

'How could I?' he says, eventually. His voice drops to a whisper and he turns to look at the sheep. 'How could any-one risk it again?' Yet, as he says this out loud, he wonders for the first time if it might be possible. And it hits him just how brave Jeannie must be. How much harder it has been for her and yet she is willing to risk it all for a second time. He sighs. The front of his shirt is soggy with tears. 'I don't know what to do,' he says, but there is no response.

And the sheep chews and stands and watches and leans. And listens. Possibly. And Reuben takes out his handkerchief again and blows his nose so loudly that the sheep jumps.

'You're a good listener, Sheep,' he says.

Then he suddenly remembers Albert. The plans he has. And he looks the sheep in the face and feels himself blushing. Has he really stolen a sheep? Really? He imagines the blood of the slaughterhouse, the cold concrete, the noise of it all and his jaw clenches.

The sheep suddenly bleats. A loud *Maaar* right in his face. Its breath smells of rotting grass. Reuben wrinkles his nose and breathes out. 'Jesus!' He pushes it away and swings his legs into the van and starts the engine.

'Well, I have to get back now, Sheep,' he says. 'Jeannie will be waiting for me.' His face smiles at the thought. At the things he might say. 'But first things first.'

He pulls out of the lay-by. He does a U-turn in the road, tyres skidding on the loose gravel, the sheep leaning hard into him, as its feet slip on the metal floor. And he heads back towards the mountains.

And the sheep looks over his shoulder, sniffing the air, its face blank as it heads for home.

Sally grew up on a farm in the north of England and worked for several years in environmental and public health. Last year her novel *Structural Damage* won the Caledonia Novel Award and it is currently in the hands of her agent Laura Williams at Greene & Heaton Literary Agency. She has an MA in Creative Writing from Bath Spa University and lives in Bristol. When not writing, she tramps along the UK's wonderful coastal footpaths.

Having the Time of My Life

by Colin Brezicki

It was silly to panic over a postage stamp. Even a little worrying at her age.

What did Matt say last time he was home? *Life's too short to sweat the nickels and dimes, Mum.* The easy mantra of a free spirit, but still.

She'd always fretted over trivial things—a forgotten birthday, an overdue bill—and now a postage stamp threatened to spoil her Cape Wrath adventure.

Yes, she should have allowed more space on the card for a larger stamp, but she wrote the address before buying it.

It was a ridiculous size for a stamp, even a special issue on the Queen's ninetieth. An archived photo of Ma'am wearing a lemon coat and sponge cake hat, smiling in an open car beside Barack Obama, he waving to the crowd and happy as Larry.

She had the card with her now, hoping to find a post office with normal stamps. But all she'd seen on the roller-coaster road from Ullapool were highland cattle and sheep, some isolated hill farms, and a gas station.

There would be nothing at Cape Wrath, though that was half the attraction of going there.

The other half was going it alone.

She could make it there and back before dark, the car rental assured her, especially this far north with the long daylight hours. Angelika, the tour chaperone, approved her going.

Gems of the Highlands were headed for John O'Groats—a touristy place that didn't top her list of attractions, despite being at the top of the country. On the way, they were to stop at castle Mey, but that didn't appeal either. It was too soon after Urquhart for another castle, especially a lived-in one. She always hung back while the group poked around inside any castle where the family still resided. When she put her own house on the market after Clayton died she disliked having to vacate her home on open days so strangers could traipse through her rooms gawking at family photos and personal effects.

Today she had cut loose from her mirthless tour companions to see Cape Wrath. The name made her think of November storms pounding a bleak coastline.

Driving north on the lonely road, she reckoned the chances of finding a post office were, like the landscape now, more remote than ever.

The card must arrive home before she did. To show up ahead of one's postcard was slipshod. Life was about shipshape and Bristol fashion, as her dear father used to say. *A place for everything, wee Grace, and everything in its place.* And due dates observed. She hadn't been a university librarian for nothing.

The card was perfect. She found it in the shop at Urquhart Castle, a striking photo of the spectacular ruins etched against the deep blue of Loch Ness under a moonstone sky. Liz and Ken would be pleased to imagine her touring the castles of Scotland in glorious weather. Their retirement gift.

A bus tour was never her choice, but Urquhart had stirred something, no question.

For starters, the weather was anything but glorious. She had stood transfixed above the ruins watching a magnificent storm move up Loch Ness. Its dark sleeves hung like a weeping cypress, draping the hills and blackening the waters as it approached.

The group dashed inside the visitors' centre when they felt the first fat drops; but Grace zipped up her anorak, yanked the hood over her head and descended the wooden staircase to the castle. The storm soon shrouded the ruins, giving the scene a melancholy aspect as she picked her way along the broken walls. It felt oddly exhilarating to be there alone in the rain.

On the bus afterwards, Myra Gladstone said to her, 'You look like a drowned rat, Grace. Did no one ever tell you to come in out of the rain?' Then she looked around, smirking at the others.

Myra was quick to establish herself as the group's mother hen during the meet-and-greet at Toronto International. Grace could imagine her at school, haranguing the meek and uncertain, making life miserable for anyone who resisted her will. Her husband, a tall, tailored man with a sweep of white hair and a rueful expression, had been something in hedge funds. Myra assured everyone they had done very well thank you.

The rest were a prickly lot, mostly. The way they competed over their grandchildren—little prodigies, every one—and their own busy-busy social lives, the charities they quilted and biked and baked for now they were retired.

Smartphones would come out, the photos stroked and tapped and shared, but the proud smiles tightened a little when it became someone else's turn.

Their husbands stared out at the hills, mostly, or nodded off in their seats. A coach tour wouldn't have been Clayton's cup of tea either.

Grace sat with Inara Di Franco, because she too liked to gaze out at the still lochs and the hills yellowed bright with gorse.

Among challenging types like Myra Gladstone, Grace made herself disappear, like this morning, slipping away to Cape Wrath.

Anyone seen Grace since breakfast? Inara Di Franco would ask, and Angelika would tell them. She wouldn't be missed.

Making herself invisible was a skill she acquired during her forty-year marriage to Clayton. Invisible but never idle. Something else she owed her father.

She did the lion's share of raising Liz and Matt while working full-time at the McLuhan Library. Clayton, for his part, paid the hefty school fees from his substantial salary. He flew business class across the country, selling technology and riding high on back-slapping camaraderie at executive retreats and marketing summits. He cut a dashing figure with his expensive suits and easy charm, but those hand-made Italian shoes could run roughshod over his competitors—and poor Matt, who seemed to disappoint his father whatever he did.

Clayton wasn't much impressed by Grace's employment either, and once joked that her own shelf life would soon expire. She thought the marriage was in trouble, but he meant libraries.

'Books are done, Grace. It's screen, not page anymore. Unless you upgrade you'll be left behind.'

Sure enough, she was blindsided when the University Board approved a complete makeover for the McLuhan. Bookcases to be replaced by a user-friendly space with computer hubs and wide screens, and a student café where lattés trumped silence as the order of the day.

'What'd I tell you, Hon?'

Yet, it was *his* demise—how sadly ironic—that ensured her early retirement and enabled her to walk away from a library without books.

Now this wild, impromptu charge up the coast to Cape Wrath. So impulsive, so unlike her.

Mum, be sure to send us a card, okay?

She hadn't written anything important; one never did on a postcard. It was the sending that mattered. Letting family know they were in one's thoughts.

Having a lovely time. In Edinburgh, I found Spottiswood Road where Father grew up. Silly me, I had a little cry when I saw the house. Then Oban and now Ullapool. Castles everywhere! Weather amazing, just like Urquhart in the pic. Forever grateful. Love and hugs to Arn and Bub. Gram. XO.

What names now. All stripped down to monosyllables. Apt, somehow, with everyone too rushed to spell things out anymore. Those ciphers in Liz's text messages— sentences clipped like a telegram. At least a telegram communicated something important. Anyway, names had shortened with the times. Matt. Liz. Ken. Arn. Bub.

Bub isn't short for anything, Mum. We just like the name.

Thankfully, Grace was irreducible.

Though *Gram* now.

She wasn't comfortable with *Gram*. She didn't know how to be *Gram* because little Arn and Bub always seemed keen for her to leave almost the minute she arrived, so they could get back to their devices. They had long lost interest in the stories she read to them and, yes, that was natural at their age, but even when she asked them to show her the games they played on their devices they became impatient. The thought occurred—and she wished it hadn't—that they were glad she'd been sent away.

You'll have a fabulous time, Mum. You'll make lovely new friends. And you had a rough ride before Dad died.

That was true enough. After as well. The sharp guilt rose now like reflux. She had wished *him* away in the end. Every day she spent in ICU holding his damp, spongy hand, staring at the blips on the monitors and pretending he even knew she was there, was another day lost.

And then that evening when she spoke those terrible words—more to herself than to his comatose form, but still. 'Do you suppose you might let go anytime, Clayton? Don't you think you'd be better off?'

And the shock when he died an hour later. Flat-lined just like that. The doctors had their own explanation, but he had heard her, she knew. Somewhere inside that disease-bloated body he heard her ask him to let go. And for once he obliged.

Matt took it harder than Liz, surprisingly. He never seemed to miss his father when he was away, and he kept his distance when Clayton was home; yet at the service he was almost inconsolable.

He was in Moldova now, or was it Azerbaijan—an unstable country regardless—riding his Vespa and living off what work he could find. He came home that one time when Grace sent him the fare. But after two weeks he grew restless and headed back to wherever he'd parked his scooter.

She loved her aimless, wandering Matt, but missed him in a different way now, more like a phantom limb.

He would text to tell her he was okay, puttering through a country whose location she sometimes had to look up. Did some of these places even *have* postcards, she wondered.

'Don't you want to come home and settle down? Find a job here?' she asked him during his visit.

'Wherever I am is home, Mum.' He made it sound simple. Home is where you are.

Same for molluscs, she thought. Or were they gastropods? Whatever. Creatures that carried their homes around with them.

She once read how the earliest cameras photographed only stationary objects—buildings, say, or trees—because imaging took forever. If someone walked through a scene during exposure they left no impression. Like Matt.

Kilroy was here.

Like her.

For all her family and career, what impression had *she* left after sixty years of making herself invisible? Like right now. Heading to the remotest point in the Kingdom in search of a postage stamp.

She parked at the jetty across from Cape Wrath and joined the small group awaiting the ferry. She spotted it, a simple outboard, slicing through the water from the opposite shore.

She paid the ferryman, a laconic old salt, and took a seat in the stern.

The group included a blond, Nordic-looking couple, he with ice-blue eyes and perfect teeth, she with a tattoo of musical notes trickling down her neck. A paunchy man in a Red Sox cap squeezed in beside his possum-faced wife who kept eyeing the high water. A slim, elderly man with a creased, narrow face sat in front staring back at the jetty like he was having second thoughts.

No one conversed over the wail of the engine. She watched the gulls wheel above the boat as it troughed the surface on its way across the kyle. A yellow minibus waited to take them to the headland.

During the bone-shaking ride across the moor, Eric their driver delivered his spiel on Cape Wrath. *Most remote part of the British mainland—army artillery site—spectacular views—'Wrath' from the Norse meaning 'turning place'—Viking ships turned at the headland and headed home.*

Nothing to do then with November storms hammering the coastline.

An hour's drive took them to the rim of the world: a lone lighthouse, two naafi huts and the abyss beyond.

Eric led the others into the canteen hut. The minibus stood empty, shimmying in the gusts.

Leaning into the gale, she climbed the grassy slope to the cliff edge. Turning her face to the sea she raised a hand to shield her eyes against the wind. It tugged at her lashes and roared in her ears. Above the rush she heard the *clink clink* of the rope ties banging against the metal flagpole and looked up to see the blue and white Saltire snapping in the wind. The whitewashed tower lit up whenever the sun broke through. Far below, gulls cried and reeled on the crosswinds that swept in from the sea.

To the north she could see Orkney, suspended between sea and sky, and to the east, Dunnet Head, a dark leviathan brooding on the wrinkled surface.

She stood for a time, her mind vacant, then turned to look across the grassy moor at the world she had come from. Somewhere to the right was her daughter's family—but what were their names? How absurd not to remember. *Liz*, of course. And husband Ken. The boys, Arn and Bud.

Looking left she imagined where Azerbaijan might be. Matt riding his Vespa, alone or with a friend. She hoped with a friend.

The party emerged chattering from the canteen and walked up the rise to where she stood. Then everyone grew silent and gazed out to sea, surrendering to the emptiness.

Inevitably, the phones came out and selfies taken against the lighthouse. Red Sox and the possum woman posed solemnly, his phone extended on a stick like he was toasting a marshmallow. The Nordic couple laughed when they looked at their photo. The elderly man aimed his camera at Dunnet Head, now luminous in a bright sun.

Grace hadn't thought to bring hers.

Stepping away, she opened her purse and took out the postcard. She unfolded her wallet and, finding the stamp, peeled off its backing and stuck it on, covering the address. Raising her arm she held the card up to the wind.

When she let go, it seemed to hang for an instant as if uncertain what to do. Then a gust snatched it away and it vanished in the glare. Airmailed at last.

She smiled.

The possum woman looked away.

Eric suggested a photo before they drove back. Grace positioned herself between the elderly man and the girl with the musical tattoo. Eric took their email addresses so he could send them Cape Wrath moment.

A turning point.

On the ride back, half-listening to Eric talk about Orkney myths, she heard him mention *selfies* and wondered what cellphones had to do with Celtic folklore. When he elaborated on the magical seals that once came ashore to be transformed into young women, she realized he said *selkies*.

Gazing out at the moorland she felt her heart race with a new excitement she couldn't explain.

She would forward the photo to Matt when she got back to Ullapool.

Colin Brezicki is a member of the Writers' Union of Canada and winner of the J.K. Galbraith fiction prize (2014). He has published two novels *A Case for Doctor Palindrome* and *All That Remains* while his short fiction has been acknowledged internationally. He was recently longlisted for the CBC Fiction, and Commonwealth Writers, contests and was runner-up for the 89th Writers Digest fiction prize (2020). His website is www.colinbrezicki.com.

In real life Colin is a retired English teacher/ theatre director who enjoys music, reading, cycling and residing in the wine region of Niagara. And of course, he has a cat.

Whale Watching

by Diana Powell

She was standing on the headland when the whale came into view. Dishrag white, a floating giant barnacle. The man was spread cross-like on its flank, caught in a cat's cradle of harpoon hemp. There was no-one else to see it, only her. She had started running as soon as it left the harbour; she knew the way. The creature turned towards her, watching her from its one pig-eye; the man looked, too. And then it turned again, facing the open sea.

The man waved to her, as they disappeared into the mist, towards Ireland.

'Goodbye,' she said, waving back.

When she told, toothless gums nah-nahed at her, hands came together and trapped her in a corner of the school-yard. Names boxed her ears.

'Thicko!'

'Fibber!'

'Twpsin!'

'Liar, liar...'

And yes, next day, at the harbour, the whale was there

again, and the waving man was walking about, talking to the crowd.

'There!' her teacher told her. 'You mustn't make things up! That's what films are for!'

'Miss' spent her Saturdays at the Palace in the big town. 'We must visit the *set* as often as we can,' she told the school. 'It will be an educational experience.' She brought *movie* magazines into class, and showed them pictures of the *stars*. One day, she brought the book, which had the same name as the film. 'It's too old for all of you, but I shall read you some.'

'Call me Ishmael,' she began. It was enough.

She told them how brave the whale-hunters were, how many useful things came from whales.

They lived in Wales, didn't they? The children scratched their heads.

'Margarine. So much better than butter, so much easier for cooking! Oil. Potions for your mothers' lotions and make-up. Where would we be without them?'

They made models out of newspaper, water and flour. The boys put them in puddles and watched them sink.

Whenever they visited Lower Town, where the filming took place, teacher's legs grew longer and shinier. Her lips were red against pale, pillowed cheeks, beneath coils of hair, stacked like lobster-pots. She edged the children towards the *stars*, careless of the water, the *lens* of the camera. The *director* motioned them away, the teacher's cheeks reddened, even through their whale-oil glaze. Yet they still went back the next day.

Weeks later, after the film *crew* had gone, and the coast

was quiet once more, she climbed to the headland again. Far below, pieces of rotting carcass were washed along the shore; caught amongst the jagged outcrops, floating in the rock pools, along with a pink hair-slide. Later still, she saw a group of seals playing with scraps of white flesh, passing them from nose to nose, smiling.

And there was blood, she was certain there was blood... spreading strands like dulse seaweed... on the seals, on the rocks. How could there be blood if it wasn't real?

She knew what she had seen, and if she had seen it, it must be true.

Soon, the people of the town forgot, going back to their fishing and farming; waiting for holiday-makers who never came. In time, another film came along, with new actors. Brighter stars in even bigger cars, who stayed longer; who were Welsh, like them, and drank in the pub, rather than the big hotel; drank in the pub again and again. Other things were different, too. Cameras taking photos of cameras, televisions in every house, some of them in colour. (Marriage.) Phones in every house, to make gossiping easier; cars in every drive, making the world smaller. (Children.) Soon the old film was forgotten. Only she remembered. Remembering, as she dredged nappies through bleach-water, her hands as wizened as the whale. As her husband snored beside her. As she wrote her name in the dust on the shelf, where the book lay. She had bought it she didn't know when... or perhaps when the librarian told her one too many times 'you've borrowed this before!'

A heavy book, as heavy as the creature, full of weighty

words, that she couldn't understand, meanings she could never fathom. The Whale meant something. The Hunt meant something. But what? And the teacher had lied when she said it began with 'Call me Ishmael'. Page after page must be got through before that, lines, paragraphs speaking of Leviathans, and Spermacetti, and Right and Orks. How they killed, or were killed. Of their bones and teeth decorating the land.

There was no Great White, the white came later, in the story proper. She drew the book out, from where it stood, amongst thinner, lighter tales of nurses and doctors in love, or Cowboys fighting Indians. She wanted to read it, but the alien words floundered in her head, 'hypos/Manhattoes/circumambulate flailing against the children's crying and squabbling, and her husband's complaining. She put it back in its place.

And soon it didn't matter that she couldn't read it. The film came back to her, in a little plastic box she must post beneath the television. She could watch it again and again, while the family yakked and pulled and grew around her. All she had to do was press a button, and rewind.

When the famous actor died, the local paper printed his picture, writing about his visit to their little town. Scrunching her eyes over her glasses, the points of her scissors laboured around the article, with her thickened knuckles, her stiff thumb. She put the piece in her special box, with all her other cuttings, yellowed by the years.

'I met him,' she told anyone who would listen. 'He put his hand on my head, tangling my hair.' She was afraid for her new pink slide. Her mother had rowed her for losing the old one on the cliffs. The day she had seen the whale.

'Call me Ahab,' he said, his voice dragging his words, low. There was something wrong about that... If he was Ahab, there would be only one long black pleated leg facing her. There would be a white line cloven down his face. He wouldn't smile, which he did, before moving back through the crowd.

Later, he appeared on the step of the trailer, his cheek forked like lightning. His wooden leg caught between the treads. She was glad. It made sense again.

'The whale bit it off at the knee,' someone in the crowd whispered. 'It's not wood,' another voice added. 'It's the bone of a whale.'

'It's not bone... it's...'

Whatever it was, *he* was as he should be... if he was Ahab. Until he smiled at her again.

Her teacher shot slit-eyes at her and pulled her away.

'I know, now, that it was jealousy. I didn't understand then.' Perhaps she should have left her story there. But no, the words spilled out of her mouth, bubbling up, as she told how she had seen the whale, far out to sea, with the actor strapped to its side.

There was no name-calling any more, but faces turned away, hands lifted to stop sniggering breath. People in the market, her children. Not her husband; he, too, was dead by then.

'You're muddling what you think you saw with the ending of the film,' Mari, her daughter, told her.

How did *she* know? She hadn't been born then; she herself

was only a child, a small child. Had she ever seen the film? 'Only a million times, when we were growing up!'

'Look!' she said to no-one in particular; Mari, who had already walked away, her dead husband, an empty room, showing them another photo from her box, one she had cut from a film magazine, when her fingers moved more easily. 'There! That's me!'

And it was; a girl, of about five, with her fringe pulled back by a slide; pink, it would be if there was colour. A girl with a Peter Pan collar, and Mary Jane shoes. A pleated skirt, with a pin in it. She was standing at the front of the crowd, on the edge of the quay. That was the first day of filming, before the visits with school.

Her fisherman grandfather had gone there early, hearing they may want him – or his boat – and he had taken her. So she was there, at the very beginning, when the big, shiny cars arrived, when the ship with its three tall masts pulled into the harbour, when the hammering, shouting, dragging, lifting started, to make towers of wood for the cameras, to hide fronts of houses, to make new ones, which were old.

'See,' her grandfather said. 'Those ships are just the kind that would have berthed here last century. See, that car... you'll never see a tidier one round here.' Time chopped and churned with the tide, in front of her eyes.

'I went every day after that. Early, before school. Late, after. And then there were our visits with the teacher. That's how I'm in the photo. I was there so much, always near the front.'

That's how she was so quick to spot the whale heading out to sea. Why she was the first to run. Why only she saw it.

Time was like that now, rewinding, fast-forwarding like her video tapes. Soon, there were grandchildren to tell, to show the yellow pages. When they were small, they nodded and smiled, and said 'yes, how wonderful, Nain.' She hugged them and their words close. She put them in a different box. But they grew, too.

'Tell us about Taid, Nain,' they would say. 'Shall we look at some photos of him?' Perhaps there were some, somewhere, but she didn't know where, and her film box was always at hand.

One of them, his name just beyond reach, took the faded picture from her, looked at it near his eyes.

'This isn't here, Nain. It's in Ireland. See the signs in the street behind? And our harbour has the cliff rising above it. That can't be you.'

She looked at the picture again. The boy didn't know how the film men could change things, how they could change young men into old, and back again, legs into ivory stumps, rubbish bins into barrels, how they could paint a cliff in, or take one away.

It *was* her. She had been there.

The grandchildren came with the summer, sent for sun and fresh sea air. Yet they spent their days staring at screens, and flicked their thumbs up and down. They said you could find the whole world in a phone.

Still, if she asked, they would take her to the harbour.

There was colour, now. Blue, red, yellow painted houses. An ice-cream van. Rainbow sun-shades.

'Much better,' people said.

The film people had taken the colour away – what little there was back then. They didn't want it. Not here. They wanted drab stone, moulding wood, grimed window-panes. Cobbles. They could magic all these, as they had done with the cliff, and the signs. But it had been many years before the colour came, following the tourists, who had finally discovered the town, along with their ice-creams and crab sandwiches and boat-trips. Yes, they did that now, sleek, fast boats, out into the bay; bird-watching, dolphin-spotting, paying good money. 'No sightings guaranteed...' When they came back, she would hear their wonder. 'I saw a fin!' 'It jumped out of the water!' 'They followed us for ages!' A whale, sometimes, a small affair, and yet they made such a fuss.

What was so special about this, she asked herself? Dark curves, that could hardly be glimpsed, except through a glass. Camouflaged by the black troughs of the sea, except for those showy jumps.

Her whale moved on top of the water.

It was white, and huge.

'I've seen a whale,' she wanted to say, the words coming close to her mouth.

'I've seen a whale,' she said. 'Here, just here, and then...'

The children, or children's children, hurried her away.

On her good days, they would take her to the cliffs, where the farm had been.

'I was born here, it was my home,' she would tell them, waving towards the buildings behind her. Holiday cottages, now, 'sought after, in sight of the sea.' Yes, it was what she woke up to, every day. It was part of her. They had said the same about the story; the sea was part of it, too. The sea meant something, like those other things that were supposed to mean something.

This place, high up, looking both ways, was one of her favourites. The water did everything here, on different days, at different times. And it was where she had seen the whale disappear.

'I ran, as soon as the mooring broke free. I knew which way it would go; I knew the currents. They – the film people – followed only the marked tracks, and stumbled at each outcrop. Have I told you this before?'

She followed the beast along the coast, running from cove to cove, over the cliff tops.

'My pink hair-slide broke free and skittered down the cliff. I couldn't see above the height of the gorse, but I knew where I was going. Home. I was the one who got here first. I was the one to see the whale rounding the corner. I was the one to see it disappear, with the famous actor tied to the side.'

They always shuffled glances then, in time with their feet; their thumbs would start that fidgeting again, and they would say 'No, no!' 'It wasn't like that at all.' 'Look, it says here...'

They showed her things she didn't want to see – a picture of a white cylinder, with wires and cogs behind, a man pulling levers inside.

'Look!' They were fond of that word. And she lowered her

eyes to whatever was on the little screen. But she saw nothing, she didn't have to see, unless she wanted to.

They told her things she didn't want to hear.

There was no whole whale. Just bits – a tail, a head, sections that they moved around on a barge, putting them in the water when needed. Or... there were three models, but none of them whole...

Sixty feet, eighty-five feet, one whale, three. No whales, parts of whales, a model in a tank; a picture on a studio wall. Rubber; steel.

'An internal engine to pump the spouting water!'

'Dye in the latex skin, so that it could 'bleed'!'

'A publicity stunt, Nain! Just imagine the press coverage such a story would get.'

'Hollywood star nearly drowns, swept out to sea on the back of a whale!''

'A myth,' another announced. 'Built from half-truths, a muddle of events. Look, a section broke free; the actor nearly drowned being dunked in a tank in the studio. Then they all said different things. The coastguard sailed to the rescue! The R.A.F. was called! But none of it happened! The camera guy says this... the director says that... Gregory Peck something else entirely! But they all seem to settle on 'no whale'!'

'No,' she said. 'They must have forgotten. They had so much to do. They moved on quickly.'

They moved on to another film, another story. It became nothing to them.

The children leave with the summer. She is glad.

Soon, everything they've said is gone again. All the 'looks' bundled away, along with their forgotten names. And the whale drifts out of the harbour, great, white, whole, with the famous actor trapped in a web of twine. She runs along the cliff, her pink slide falls, and there it is again.

Soon, she sees the sea every day, just as in her childhood, in this place they've put her in, calling it 'home'. Home again, sea again.

And there are new people who listen to her story, and say 'How interesting!' Or, 'Good!' no matter how many times she tells. She cannot see the film anymore – her eyes are too dim. Besides, none of the other 'residents' want to watch it. But the nice girls will read to her from the book, if she asks, when they have the time.

It is the ending she wants to hear. How Ahab raises his hand from the flank of the whale, beckoning his crew to carry on with the kill.

'I saw it,' she tells them. 'I saw the whale disappear into the mist, with the famous actor tied to its side. He waved at me, so I said 'Goodbye.''

'No,' the girl who is reading to her that day, tells her; a girl who pays attention to the words on the page. 'Ahab gets pulled into the water. It's the Parsee who is caught on the whale. And he doesn't wave. They changed it for the film. They changed the whole ending. It's what they do, for dramatic effect.'

After the girl has gone, she puts the book in the bin.

And the whale turns towards the open sea, and the man raises his hand to her.

'Goodbye.'

Diana Powell's stories have featured in a number of competitions, such as the 2019 Chipping Norton Literature Festival Prize (winner), 2020 Society of Authors ALCS Tom-Gallon Trust Award (runner-up) and the 2020 TSS Cambridge Prize (3rd place). Her work has appeared in several anthologies and journals, including 'Best (British) Short Stories 2020' (Salt).

Her novella, *Esther Bligh*, was published in June 2018 (Holland House Books). Her collection of stories, *Trouble Crossing the Bridge* came out in 2020.

Her novella, *The Sisters of Cynvael* won the 2021 Cinnamon Press Literature Award, and will be published next year.

She has a website https://dianapowellwriter.com and can be found on FaceBook and Twitter (@diana_p_writer).

Poppin' Down the Chippie

by Steve Atkinson

She stepped out lightly onto the pavement, alone and some-how regal. There was nobody about, no pedestrians, no traf-fic, and she tripped along, carefree, upright and purposeful. The street was hers; an empty domain of concrete and tar-mac, lamp-posts and shop fronts with coloured awnings. The first window offered a tempting orgy of assorted delights; humbugs, sherbet lemons, pink and white flying saucers and multi-layered gob-stoppers big enough to choke a blue whale. She stopped to peer for a while, and old Mrs Henderson gave her a cheery wave from behind the counter, beckoning her inside. She shrugged and smiled back, mouthing 'must-get-to-the-chippie' as she jabbed a finger towards the end of the street. Mrs Henderson feigned a sad face and returned to a slab of toffee she was pummelling with a light, silver hammer.

The girl in the pink summer dress turned away, a mild re-luctance in her gait. Next door was a hardware store and next to that a pharmacy. Little to interest her there. She skipped on, listening to the sounds of her own ringing footsteps as she recalled street games she played when she was even younger;

jacks, hop-scotch and 'avoid-the-cracks'. If you stepped on one, the bears would get you. Or worse!

The village High Road was bright and sunny but she was the only one about. She hugged herself in delight at the sense of warmth and well-being in the sunlight. She could climb a mountain, swim any sea. Her heart was as light as the crimson ribbon in her long wavy hair. It was good to be alive. She would like to go to the rec, to play on the climbing frame and swings, but she had to get to the chippie. It was a perfect summer's day for it, but she was on a mission.

Just past the bright red post-box she bent to pet a little Scottish terrier.

'What's the matter with you?' she cooed. 'Why aren't you at home in your garden? It's not safe for a doggie to be out on his own in the street.'

She ruffled his ears. 'Now shoo off home,' she gently chided and stood to continue her journey. Slightly troubled, she remembered how her mother would scold *her* for petting a dog before food, even chips.

Her melodic voice rang in her ears as she skipped along her way. 'Wash your mitts, evict the nits.' She smiled and carefully wiped her fingers on her dress. 'There!' she declared. 'Clean as a whistle.'

Just as she came to the tiny red-brick police house PC Williams was stepping out to begin his patrol.

'Well, hello, little one,' he said, his deep sonorous voice reminding her of her father's, before the war. 'Off to the chippie?' She grinned up at him, and wondered if she should curtsy as she was often to do when she met strangers. But the policeman wasn't a stranger so she just waved as she passed.

'Don't cross the road without looking,' he called after her, although he knew there would be no need for her to cross any road. Besides, there was no traffic.

Next to the police house with its old-fashioned blue lamp was Mrs Jacobs' cottage and, beyond that, the toy shop. Here she was sorely tempted inside although she had barely enough money for the chips. She stopped to stare in the window. Teddy bears, dolls, model trains and even a brightly coloured jack-in-the-box begged her affectionate attention. She pulled a sad face as Mr Carver beckoned her in, his spectacles sticking out from a breast pocket in his white coverall coat. She pursed her lips again to silently mouth: 'Got-to-get-to-the-chippie.'

She knew that he was just faking the teardrop wiped delicately from his eye, but she yielded and with girlish joy thrilled to the familiar chimes as she opened the door.

'I think I might have just the thing for you,' Mr Carver said solicitously, leaning behind him to produce a gleaming blue and red spinning top. 'This one hums as it spins.'

He leaned over the counter and pressed the wooden grip to set it in motion and she positively melted at the soothing sounds that accompanied its whirring wobble.

'New in today,' he said. 'It's going to be all the rage. Not even tin, but bright modern plastic. Do you like it?'

Her eyes already told him all he wanted to know. Her hands were clasped delightedly at her front, almost as if she were in prayer.

'I don't have the money,' she said. 'I've got to get to the chippie.'

No, silly,' Mr Carver said, kindly. 'Tell your mother this is a marketing sample. The manufacturers want to know whether children will like it, not being of tin and all that.'

'Marking sample?' Now her eyes were nearly popping out of her head.

'A sort of free trial – but for keeps,' he insisted. 'And in a week or two you can tell me how you got on with it. You don't have to return it. You are doing the makers a sort of favour.'

But she knew she couldn't accept it, at least not without her mother's permission. 'I'll tell mummy,' she said. 'Perhaps she'll bring me back. Thank you.'

Mr Carver smiled sadly as she turned to leave. 'Have you seen my glasses?' he enquired jovially, slapping his hands against his sides to check his coat pockets. 'I've mislaid my glasses.'

'Top pocket,' she replied, pointing, and left the shop giggling to the wondrous sound of musical chimes as the door opened again.

She was nearly there. Just another few steps and already she could smell the vinegar and batter, saveloys and mushy peas, and her mouth watered as she imagined her chips casually wrapped in yesterday's *Daily Sketch*.

Outside the chippie stood that young rascal Tom Scaggs, his hands deep in the pockets of his hand-me-down trousers. She couldn't actually remember seeing him in any other pose.

'Where you goin'?' he ventured sulkily. 'Ain't you got your mum wiv' yuh?'

'Do I look as if I have my mother with me?' she answered haughtily. 'Kindly step aside, Tom Scaggs. I'm going in for chips.'

'Chips? 'Ere, can I 'ave some? I'm famished.'

'And what will you do for me, Tom Scaggs?' She knew better than to give the likes of him something for nothing.

'I've got a big, fat glass marble, with more swirling colours than a summer sunset.'

'Can't eat a marble,' she said. 'I'm hungry, too.'

'Just three chips,' he implored. 'It's a bargain, that is. Pleeeaase, Alice.'

'We'll see,' she insisted, mysteriously, as she stepped round him. 'You hum a bit.'

'You, too,' he said, swirling round to watch her enter the chippie. In a quieter tone he added: 'Quite nice really... roses, or summat. Definitely flowers.'

'Well, I don't wear scent,' she admonished. 'But someone I could touch with a short stick ought to.'

He pulled a hurt face but beneath her imperious façade she was smiling warmly.

That Tom Scaggs, she thought. *What a deadbeat!*

There was a new man behind the counter, someone she didn't at first recognise. A large leonine head and a white coat, just like Mr Carver, but in his breast pocket, not spectacles, but the tops of two shiny red pencils.

'Hello, Alice,' he said, which surprised her. 'Sixpennyworth?'

She nodded, slightly confused. 'Where's Mr Davies?'

You know me, Alice,' he said with an apologetic, regretful smile. 'I'm Dr Wilson.'

'But...?'

'She's gone,' announced Dr Wilson quietly, gazing down at Alice's frail, elderly head on the pillow. Gently, respectfully, he let go of the taper-thin wrist he had been monitoring as her pulse faded. Her frozen expression was soft with undisguised contentment. He took one of the bright red pencils from his pocket and, checking his watch, recorded the TOD on a clipboard. He turned to a forlorn looking figure still holding her right hand on the other side of the bed. 'My deepest condolences, Mr Scaggs. But she looks as if she slipped away with some very happy memories.'

Stephen Atkinson, 74, has been a roving reporter, sub editor, columnist, news editor and deputy editor throughout his working life, finally retiring after 30 years on the Daily Mirror. He has since written half a dozen books, mostly short story collections except for one novella called *Ludec*, a sci fi twist on the Battle of Hastings.

Last Mother's Day

by Eamonn Kirk

I climb the stairs, carpet threadbare, with tripping slippage and deafening pattern. I am careful, hushed in each repeated step. Descended the night before at speed, in sleeping bag or cardboard box. For when you, cat, were away, we mice did play. Enough toast to burn the house down, and tea to drown China. Watching grown-up TV, scary adult crap I wouldn't entertain now. I don't remember nightmares, but surely those tales burrowed deep as mind worms, settling in for the dark's duration. Dad around, doing his own distant thing in the room next door, but could have been down the street, or half a world away.

Often we wake early, whirlwinding dervishly, spiriting away the past evening's present carnage. Washing-up mountains scaled and razed. Clothes stuffed away in tight, sulky balls, with furniture set back to the walls. Books and papers lined up to attention, keenly waiting to be read again. All alert to the sound of knocking, in case once again, you've forgotten your key, perhaps ambivalent towards the return. The only time we use the front door, why is that? As if coming or going is shameful, so deeply private as to be kept hidden, like damp knickers on a washing line.

I have no hand on the banister, but a firm grip on your cuppa. Your reward for a distant night of care for the hips, the eyes, the strokes, the God knows what's wrong with them. I accept you're borrowed for a time, but I don't quite like it. I think you love nursing as much as mothering. Maybe more. You in a long line of immigrants propping up the nation's health, with children everywhere orphaned for a while.

The air is thick with soupy steam. I never wonder at our Sunday dinner. Quick and easy, lunch from a can. Never enough, but comfortingly predictable. The mock disgust at mixing chicken and tomato, a pan of liquid brown that still did the trick. The rare surprise of mushroom, creamy and unpolluted by anything else. White bread, full of air, gobbled at speed to make us hiccup. Then maybe a trip to a dilapidated park, or the crumbling seafront. Always a split decision, always somewhere fading away from glory.

It gets us out, and away from the missing of you. The park is slowly falling apart, and everywhere drips graffiti, fag ends, and piss. Still there are good times to be had.

The sea though is my favourite. Alive when even the shops and arcades are shut up, silent and dead. The tide takes away an ache I cannot locate.

On the edge of the prom, we are way too close. We want to get soaked for the joyful drama, the crying at ourselves and each other, while we laugh in waves. Always with ice-cream or candyfloss. One day I look over at Dad. I have finished my 99 before him. It's then that I first feel like a man.

Every Sunday, though, I come back to earth with a bump. I cry, a despair that sinks my short body down onto broken skin knees, into pitch clodding earth.

Only years later, when I can spend months not seeing you, do I get it. Each night away was a miniature death. Not like a rehearsal, where over time, I might become immune to the grief. This was the real thing, salt and vinegar in wrist slits, or wanton knee descabbing. You were gone and not there. Might never come back.

Yet here you are again, returned, under a mountain of itchy orange and brown. It's the 1970s, no pastel quilts to fluff up the beds of this decade. I imagine you a mole under a giant, garish hill, and I venture near so mousily. It doesn't matter if you're asleep; you prefer it cold, no sugar. How strangely un-Irish, but how very Catholic. Then you always toed that line, except when you felt like bucking a trend. I've never quite got used to your need to blend in, yet still keeping a rebel beat in your heart.

You stir, muttering about chasing chickens. I chuckle, as you are mid-dream. Maybe you are back home, where as a kid, you sometimes rang their necks. For a flash, I am your Daddy, ever long lost to you. Caressing a cup of nurture, laughing at your childish, runaway stories, tucked in deep under cosy heaps of blanket. But no, I am a boy of ten, and not able to quite make sense.

So I leave your tea to cool, as you like it. You'll stir eventually, take a sip, no doubt double flooded with dread of having not slept enough, and guilt of being too long away from us. While I am probably off crying under pillows, the only clear reason being it's Sunday, and that's what I do. Rise, tidy, mass, soup, park, seaside, cup of tea, cry. Over and over.

Yet today really is the end of it all. You would do it on a Sunday, of course, to put us to the least trouble. The phone rang out with news of your passing, as one day I knew it would. I have driven fearlessly to reach you. All a bit too late, but I need to see you where you belong. A brief caress downstairs with the tribe that have gathered, then I climb those stairs again, gently, so as still not to wake you.

And there you lie, under a floral duvet, as peaceful as I have ever seen. Did I ever really see you? Your mighty, coursing wrinkles have retreated. Skin is paler now, and lips carry a dash of lilac. You are borrowed for good, as slowly you descend before my eyes into a pool of skinny flesh and aching bones, no more the you I know. But I do not cry, and feel no sadness, not yet. A quick peck on your forehead, and then I retreat. Back downstairs to put the kettle on.

Eamonn Kirk has been into creative writing since he was a kid. He has amassed a small body of non-fictional work, writing on subjects as far afield as running, obesity, grief, mental health and identity, although his favourite form is fictional prose. Aside from working in the NHS as a genetic counsellor, he loves running marathons, playing piano, singing and writing. Having been grown in Lancashire, he has been firmly replanted in Wales, and lives in lovely Neath with partner

Neil, and Toby the cat. Contact details: kirk_eamonn@hot-mail.com.

Kenny, Winking

by Annie Dawid

Mom

Usually I nap every day around 2:30, before I take the younger kids to sports. The three oldest are in high school now, so no more home schooling for them. We let them choose in ninth grade. But Kenny and Christine were doing their normal routine; once a week, they do target practice out back, weather permitting.

I can sleep through anything. Over the years, I've never been bothered by probably hundreds of afternoons of target practice when the older kids were home schooling, then all through the Kenny and Christine years – there's an eight-year-gap between the youngest and oldest. If there's no wind, they get out the rifles and pin up the targets on a hay bale and practice for a half-hour. That's how we've always done it.

But that day, something woke me just as I'd entered a hazy dream, where I was in a room without any lights.

Boom!

It wasn't like any gunshot I ever heard in my life. Since I hunt, or used to, along with my husband and father and siblings and of course the kids, I've heard hundreds, maybe thousands of shots fired. But this sound was like an explosion inside my body, like the inside of a volcano deciding to erupt. Then I heard Christine scream.

Christine

He was still using the kid-size rifle that belonged to Gramps and Dad before him, and then of course the rest of us. We all did; it was a rite-of-passage when we graduated to adult-size rifles. Kenny said he was ready for the grown-up size, because he would be eleven on his next birthday. Dad said maybe. Kenny hadn't gone through a major growth spurt yet. He was smaller than most of the kids on his soccer team.

We were in the back, shooting, like always. When Kenny said he was going to the basement to get more bullets, I just nodded. It wasn't out of the ordinary to forget to bring the box up. I kept shooting, with one perfect bull's eye that surprised even me. I'm the best shooter at 4H in my age bracket, 13 to 15.

Then there was this sound. I've cried and cried, and while everybody says it wasn't my fault, I know it was. I'm the big sister, the one who's supposed to be responsible, like my big sisters and brother were with me. I just let him go. Didn't check to make sure he'd left the rifle outside. We always re-load outside, always with me watching. All of us have taken gun-safety classes. We know how to handle guns like most people around here. He'd reloaded that kid's rifle I don't know how many times, always without any trouble.

Now I understand the boom was the sound of the shot in the basement, echoing. I never heard a bullet go off *inside* a house before: mine or anyone else's. Our family has always shot outdoors: at targets, deer, and, when we're lucky in the annual lottery, elk. None of us has ever been to an indoor shooting range. I'd never heard that sound before in my life.

Travis

My twin sister and me were running track, like we do every spring. I do the 800, she does the 400, and we race each other, though the coach doesn't like it, since we're in different events. We're outside, feeling the dirt beneath our track shoes – we love that feeling after a winter of no running. It's a fantastic day: no wind, no clouds; then we hear sirens. My dad, uncle, cousins – most of the guys in our family – are all volunteer firemen. I'll join them as soon as I can, so I'm always alert to the different tones. The long, deep, uninterrupted siren is for fires. The three-beep short, high tones are for EMT only. Often you hear both, the long one first. So when I heard the three beeps starting out, I relaxed, knowing that Dad or Uncle Ted wouldn't be going out. No one's ever gotten killed fighting fires in my family, but we've had injuries. None of us does EMT, which is weird, because you actually get paid for that. But we've lived in this valley a long time: running cattle, building, fixing tractors – lots of different but important work – so we're established. Being on the force is tradition.

When the three beeps sound, T looks at me worried; then her expression changes. Good, Dad's *not* going – and then we both run faster. I let her get ahead, then zoom past at the last second before her finish line.

Tina

I always hold my breath when I hear the sirens. I want to be a firefighter too, like the guys. My dad says sure, why not? But Mom doesn't want me to. She's pretty old-fashioned some-times, though she grew up on Granddad's ranch, doing all the roping and branding and everything men did – even gelding – but after she married Dad and started making babies, she said she realized how important it was for a woman not to harm her body, especially the baby-making parts. She let's T do the training, but I can't until I'm eighteen. Two more years.

After the three beeps, I let out the air I didn't realize I'd been holding. During certain times of year, the sirens go off once a day; then weeks will pass without a single emergency. Good weather usually means no car accidents. Once, Great Aunt Betty was driving down the canyon in the rain and went over the edge, where there's no guardrail. In a coma for nine days, but she's a tough old goat, and recovered totally.

Tough women, that's what I come from. When I felt glad Dad wouldn't be going to a fire, I had another weird feeling pass through me, like a shudder, but I pushed it away, because I want to be tough. At least as tough as T, so I ran faster and harder.

Dad

My brother and me were pouring a foundation for one of the new Amish families. We've made money since they started moving here a few years back. Don't get me wrong – they're fine, upstanding Christians like us – but sometimes it rubs me the wrong way how they call attention to themselves. The way they dress and get around town, their old-fashioned clothes and the out-of-control beards and the buggies and the bicycle carts... we're Mennonite. Our people settled here in the nineteenth century, but the Amish just showed up in the early 2000s, leaving rising land prices in Ohio. Usually, our altitude scares people away, and the growing season is very short. Anyway, we're pouring when I hear the siren. Our equipment gets pretty loud, and though I should be wearing plugs, I don't. I motioned to Ted to take his out.

We were both on call, which is unusual, since the fire department has some kind of superstition about not having brothers fight together. We've got different schedules, but I was subbing for someone. I checked my radio in case we'd missed the call. Nothing. Then I assumed it was an EMT call, which normally doesn't concern me, but I thought about Dad. His emphysema's worse, so I worried about him for a minute, then figured it was for somebody else, so I went back to work.

Ted

Amish folk have money. Me and my brother, we couldn't

afford to build such a huge barn, but since they get each other to do the construction, they don't have to pay anyone. The Amish fascinate me. Strangers get Mennonites confused with them all the time, but we're so different. You can't tell us from the rest of the population by what we drive. I don't get why they can sit in a car being driven by a non-Amish but not drive themselves. They take advantage of technology but don't want to operate it. As I was pouring, I was thinking how we're using our equipment to pour them a state-of-the-art foundation for their old-fashioned barn put together with pegs and dovetail joints. The phone vibrates. I pull it from my pocket and see the sheriff's number, which is odd; I think about Dad, who might not have much time left. Before I can call back, the phone buzzes again. Sally the dispatcher says, 'Ted! You need to get your brother to *his* house. Go with him. Stop whatever you're doing and get there.' She's dead serious, so I know it's bad. It can't be about Dad if we're headed to Jim's.

Sheriff

My dispatcher gets me on the private line to tell me something's up at the Tremain's on First Street. Jim built that place on the piece of land I wanted twenty years ago. We haggled like two old women, but the actual old woman who owned it – the widow of my buddy Amos, or I thought he was my buddy – she decided to sell it to the younger and handsomer Tremain boy, and it's stuck in my craw ever since.

Don't have nothing against his family – that's a sweet wife, one of the Holt girls, and their five kids are great athletes, or were, I suppose I should say – but Jim, he's had one of them shit-eating grins since he was in kindergarten with my boy. Always gets what he wants, that Jimmy. Don't misunderstand me: I wouldn't wish anything like this on my worst enemy. But I'm trying to remember what I felt when I got that call, and I was almost – I don't know, maybe *pleased* that something was finally going wrong for that guy, and on the very land I'd wanted, where he and his brother put up what I'd call a mansion, like one of them trophy houses the summer people build on the hilltops out of town, ruining the view for everyone. Now I'm glad I didn't get the land, because maybe there's some kind of curse on it. Amos's widow thought so because Amos got on a horse drunk one night, went looking for a missing calf, then fell right where that house is now. Told everyone she didn't want to keep that part of the ranch.

EMT No. 1, Sue

Me, I've seen just about everything. Before we moved here from Chicago, I was an emergency room nurse downtown, and my husband was a cop. We've seen more gun deaths and murders and suicides and every kind of mayhem. Never in a million years did I think that any situation in Willits, Wyoming, could ever top what I'd already seen. I was Number 1 on the crew that month, Mary Ellen Number 2. We had that old drunk Dean as our driver, but that day he didn't reek.

When we moved here, I hadn't planned on being around any more injured or dead bodies. But retirement got boring –

I was gardening and had the horse of my dreams, two of them, actually – but after a year or two, the novelty wore off. I didn't need to work for the money. Now I wish I'd never started up EMT work, but at the time it seemed like a good idea. I've felt good about most of the work – mostly it's old men and women who need transport to the hospital an hour from here. We've had some gruesome car wrecks too, which the fire people work on with their Jaws of Life, so they tend to see mangled bodies first. The three years I've been an EMT, plus twenty-five in Chicago's ERs – none of it prepared me for that kid's death.

EMT No. 2, Mary Ellen

I like working with Sue. I'm still new – in my previous life, I was a dental hygienist. The worst thing I ever saw was a severely rotted set of teeth in this old man who'd been neglected by his family for years. Man, that stink was the worst thing I ever smelled in my life! Had to pull every tooth. But he didn't die from it.

EMT Driver, Dean

Those women have stronger stomachs than me any day. When I saw that kid's body – no, not his body, it was his head, or what was left of it, I lost my lunch. I couldn't help it. I'm supposed to be a professional; I know I'm a good driver – been driving all my life. Trucks, moving vans, even triple trailers in Oregon – you name it – but I'm not so good with people's brains being splattered all over the room. The kid was dead by the time we got there, so all our speeding made no difference. EMTs get sent, even when it's too late; we're supposed to secure the scene and register important information, assuming we get there before the sheriff, but Kenny's ending was just too much for me. Goddamn if I couldn't even hold it till I got outside. To get to that basement, you had to go into the kitchen, then take the stairs. It just come up too fast, so I barfed all over the gun cabinet. At least I didn't spray anybody. It was just me and Sue and Mary Ellen down there. The sister and the mother, they were glued to each other in the kitchen. The girl had run down, then back up after finding her brother. She wanted to keep her mother from seeing him, and I guess she'd succeeded. 'Mom, Mom, you can't go down there. Wait for Dad.' The mom put up a struggle, but I'm thinking she really couldn't have handled what I saw. 'Mom, the dispatcher said she'd find him and get him here right away.' That girl, Chris – she's pretty strong. Asked me to help hold her mom, but she'd been doing okay herself. I guess she was getting tired by then. I felt bad, because I knew I smelled like vomit, but the mom was hysterical. Hysteria can make you pretty strong. So I held onto that screaming woman until her husband showed up, which was about ten minutes later.

Arlene

I'm the oldest, closest to my folks. Sometimes I think they depend on me to keep it together when they can't. I was working on the computer, headphones clamped tight, when the librarian comes over. 'You've just been called to the office. You and all the Tremain kids. Go.'

My first thought was that Gramps had died. I took a deep breath, gathered my books and went to the office. I saw a bunch of my cousins arriving from elementary, and middle school, with my twin brother and sister racing in from track.

The secretary says there's been an emergency at home, and someone's coming to get us. That confused me, because Gramps is out at the ranch, unless maybe he was visiting Mom and something happened. Mrs. Hopkins said she didn't know what it was about, but I think she did and wasn't saying, because she looked like hell, like she knew something really bad had happened, and she didn't think it was her place to tell us. It wasn't. I understand she was doing the right thing, but at the time I was so worried I thought my heart was going to stop. Between the Tremain and Holt families, their siblings, their kids, there's a lot of us in the school system. I didn't know why all of us would be called unless it was Gramps. She kept saying, 'Just wait for your uncle to get here.' Or 'Just wait for your dad to get here,' to Ted's three kids. We were all looking at each other, confused and uncertain. Everyone kept asking, 'Are you sure it's not Gramps?' and she would shake her head and say, 'I don't think it's your grandfather, but I don't know. I don't want to say anything because I could be wrong. I got a call from the dispatcher saying I should get you together, and that Ted would come for you. That's all I know.'

Us older kids decided we should wait in the parking lot instead of making Uncle Ted park his truck and come find us, but just as I'm gathering the littlest ones – Ted's youngest is in first grade – I see him coming through the front door. I never saw a look like that on anyone's face, ever.

He says, 'Come outside, all of you,' in this very calm, very slow way, which I know has to mean the worst thing in the world must have happened, only I don't know what that could be. Did our house burn down? That was my first thought.

'There's been an accident,' he says slowly, once we're in front of the building clustered around him. He picks his youngest up and clutches her really tight. I know it's going to be bad, so I pick up the next youngest, Timmy, who's in third grade. It feels good to hold him, to be holding a sweet warm child who smells good, because I know that whatever Ted's going to say next will be more horrible than anything I can imagine. Maybe it's not the house. Mom? Has something happened to my mother?

'It's Kenny.' He takes a very deep breath and exhales slowly. 'Kenny had an accident with his rifle.'

Since he doesn't say 'Kenny's dead,' I'm guessing he's in the hospital, or on his way to the hospital. I didn't hear any sirens 'cause of my headphones, but maybe the others did. Maybe the Flight for Life helicopter is already here or on its way. I'm picturing Kenny shooting himself in the foot, because I could imagine him doing something stupid like that. The little kids are crying and saying 'Daddy, what happened? Tell us what happened.'

Ted looks at me. I can see in his eyes Kenny is dead, and he's afraid to say it. I look at the twins, hanging onto each other – I've always been a bit jealous of that closeness, the way they have each other. Even though I have four siblings, *had* four siblings, sometimes I feel alone, like I have to be in big charge of all of them, all the time, and I never have anyone to share it with. Mom has Dad, and a lot of the time, Mom seems overwhelmed, so I jump in and do things, but I try to make it like I'm just helping out – not that I need to do it because it won't get done otherwise. I don't want her to feel bad. Maybe she was too young when she had me, straight out of high school. Married the day after graduation, then I pop out eight months later.

'Where are we going?' I ask. 'I want to be with Mom.'

'Your dad is there with her. The EMTs and the sheriff are there, waiting for the coroner.'

'What's a coroner?' chorus the younger kids.

Ted starts crying and hugs his little girl, who immediately starts to sob. 'Your cousin, Kenny, he's gone. He had an accident with his gun. It was too late to save him.'

Instead of crying like the rest of us, Travis runs to the bike rack beside the school doors, picks up his bike and throws it as hard as he can, slamming it against the brick wall. After it falls, he picks it up and throws it, again and again. He doesn't say one word. Travis scares me. Only Tina can calm him down. She didn't try to stop him, though. The bike was already completely ruined after the first collision, and she understood what he needed to do to feel better.

All us kids can't fit in Ted's truck, but I have the big Ford, so between us, we got everyone in a vehicle.

Our house is two miles from school.

I pull up first. Ted has the younger ones, so he's driving more slowly. I'm usually the careful one, 'slowpoke' as my siblings call me, but I just tore out of the parking lot without thinking, and when I got to the dirt road, which has no other houses on it but ours, with a half-mile straightaway before the driveway, I just gunned it. My cousin Jessie, who's a freshman, is frozen with fear; she thinks I'm going to crash us. I can't slow down though. I can see – all of us can see – the collection of vehicles by the house. The EMT van, the sheriff's car, two other deputies' cars, the coroner's car, and some other vehicles I can't identify. I can't park where I normally do, so I just pull over as close as I can get and start running. I don't turn off the engine or shut the door – I had to get to Mom.

Minister

Over the decades, I'd like to think I've learned a little bit about what to say at funerals, and more importantly, what *not* to say. Each is different, of course, as unique as the individual who passed away. I'm eighty-one now – been ministering in Willits, Wyoming, for fifty-three years. So Kenny isn't the first child I've buried. In fact, one of the very first funerals I ever did was a boy, even younger than Kenny, who might have died a more horrible death, if you can judge such a thing. At any rate, it was a *longer* death. He'd been outside with the cattle in calving season, a very very cold March, as I recall, a seven-year-old who was the big kid in the family trying to help out 'cause his dad was ill. His mom was doing everything at the ranch plus caring for the three younger kids plus her husband, who I think, if I remember rightly, had pneumonia. Suffice to say, the boy got in the wrong pen and a huge, pregnant cow trampled him. He couldn't move, and was too far from the house for anyone to hear him, if he had enough strength to yell in the first place. Long story short, he was badly injured, and the temperature dropped. The mom fell asleep on the couch from exhaustion... that boy froze to death overnight, April 9, 1957.

But this is another generation altogether. Kenny's funeral was super high-tech compared to that boy's, when we still used the one-room church and one-room schoolhouse. For Kenny, we were in the new school gymnasium (paid for courtesy of Wyoming's oil and gas riches), and the family had put together a slide show. Every one of those shots had Kenny smiling, impish, silly – in some of them it was Halloween, and he was Darth Vader, another year Spiderman. There were pictures of him playing soccer, football, basketball, baseball, on horseback. No hunting shots, though.

It was one of those occasions where I knew to say as little as possible, to let the ceremony take its course. Which, in this case, was a long celebration of Kenny's short life. I didn't talk about how he died, or go into the theological ponderings of *why*, which sometimes mourners need to hear, want to talk about, to wrestle with, especially when it's a young person, or a freak accident is the cause, or some other situation where the death is a total surprise to everyone. Was Kenny shooting himself a freak accident? I just can't call it that, can't 'go there,' as my granddaughter at university in Laramie says. Can't. The boy had to turn the rifle in such a way as to aim it at his forehead, then pull the trigger, which is not the easiest thing to do with a rifle, even a kid-size one.

For two hours, no one said anything about Kenny's death, only his life.

Soccer Coach

I'm not from around here, which is to say, not one of the founding families. You can live here forty years, but if you weren't born here, then you're a newcomer. I came only ten years ago – now that I think of it, probably the year Kenny was born. Moved out here from Laramie, where I directed I.T. at the university for a few years. Then my parents died, leaving us quite a bit of money, and my wife said, 'Let's raise the kids in the country. We can move back to Laramie when they're ready for high school, if you want to.' Famous last words. As these things tend to go, I ended up liking it here in the wilds of Wyoming a lot more than she did. She's from Long Island, New York. We split up. Only took a year, but I stayed, 'cause I'd fallen in love with the place. Didn't make sense for the kids to have two schools, so they're with her during the week, and I get them weekends, vacations and summers. In Laramie, I had played soccer and coached it too, so I originated the first soccer team in Willits. I was surprised when there were enough kids to put together a few teams, since this is serious football territory. All the Tremains do sports. They're athletes in that family. So every single one of them got into it – every age group – to try it, at least. Kenny took to it more than the others. On the kids' team, Kenny was the smallest, though there were younger ones. In some of the towns we play are a number of migrant families, mostly from Mexico, and they're very serious about the game. In Mexico, soccer is like a religion, so the devotion is hard-core – not just the kids but their parents too. Deeply invested in winning. I don't think I'm being prejudiced when I say these teams sometimes play dirty. Sometimes it's good to play teams like that to get soft kids tougher. Most of the players in Willits are rule-followers. My kids too. And the older Tremain kids. But not Kenny.

He was a match for those Hispanic players. Went right through their legs, which he could get away with due to his size. He elbowed, butted, did anything to get the goal, and if the refs didn't see it – well, what was I going to do? I could always talk to him after the game, of course, and did. To no avail whatsoever. He liked his tough-guy image, especially being so small. A Napoleon complex in a ten-year-old, over-sized in his ambition to compensate for being little. He loved winning, and he loved applause. When he made a goal, with all that extended family on both sides, there was always a crowd. I think his parents and aunts and uncles and grand-parents must not have known the rules of soccer – it was new to them – so they couldn't tell when he was fouling on pur-pose, playing the dirtiest soccer out there. I'm just guessing about that, since the Tremain family seem like rule-followers; their kids don't cheat at other sports.

The strangest thing when I heard about how Kenny died was that *it didn't surprise me.*

Now that's very odd, not to be shocked by a ten-year-old

boy's death resulting from a rifle re-loading accident. I was horrified, but in no way surprised.

Around here, people don't think twice about the lethality of guns – they port 'em all over the place, right out in the open, gun racks in every truck. Growing up in San Diego, I was always drawn to the idea of the 'West,' in quotes. Living on the West Coast is *not* living in the West. When I got out of school, I could've gotten any kind of tech job I wanted. But I had this dream to be in the land of cowboys and mountain men and horses and women wearing tight jeans and boots. I never thought about the gun part of the Wild Wild West, which was a giant oversight: a key element to leave out of the myth. Unfortunately I can be like that: blind to the obvious. Like what happened with Ilene. Since we split up, I've tried to notice more, to work on observing what's around me at all times so as never to be blindsided like that again. What happened with Kenny – I'm not saying I have the answers, and I'd never voice this idea aloud in Willits, Wyoming, a place I love for its austere beauty and the sky and the clouds and the wildlife. I wouldn't want to jeopardize my position here as a newcomer, and I've heard stories – plenty of 'em – about newcomers being 'run out of town,' even after twenty years or more, for going against the accepted grain of how reality is perceived in this part of the world.

Kenny thought the rules didn't apply to him. Not in soccer. Not in regular old behavior either. I'd see him acting all loudmouth with his family, but they always called him cute, or funny, and laughed at his antics. I'm not saying he wasn't funny – he was. Since his death, I keep picturing him doing this comic routine with a toy rifle, looking down the barrel, grinning, winking, pulling the trigger and laughing when nothing happens, doing a Chaplin-esque pantomime. In my strange imagination, he smiles at me and looks like we're sharing a secret, which we often did when I saw him make an illegal move on the field and the refs didn't call it. He'd wink at me, raise his hands together like a boxing champ, bow, and run back out in the field, his family and the others chanting his name.

Annie Dawid's unpublished novel, *Paradise Undone: A Novel of Jonestown,* just won the Screencraft Cinematic Book Award for 2022. Her three volumes of fiction are: *York Ferry: A Novel,* Cane Hill Press, 1993, second printing, winner of the 2016 International Rubery Award in Fiction, *Lily in the Desert: Stories,* Carnegie-Mellon University Press, 2001 and *Darkness Was Under His Feet: Stories of a Family,* Litchfield Review Press, 2009.

Mrs Brooker

by Jane Branson

The photographer was due at eleven o'clock. At just after seven, Mrs Brooker stepped along the red-brick path, her fingers folded around her secateurs. The distant end of the garden was bright, the sun glinting off the greenhouse. But the rosebed was still in shadow, the flowers dewy, the largest blossoms bowing low, their faces wide and beseeching.

Sixty years ago, it was, that her father showed her how to find the first leaf below each spent flower, place the blades just so, make the cut clean and sharp. 'Then a new bud can grow,' he told her. She could see him still, crouching on the grass, nodding encouragement, his eyes kind. She could see herself, a ribbon in her hair, lips pressed together in her serious way, placing the snipped stem in his open palm.

She stroked a still-sealed bud, sunshine yellow squeezing to a peachy tip, creamy white fading to deep pink. At this time of year, the summer days still long, dead-heading was an almost daily job.

The sun crept across the lawn and warmed the back of her legs.

She should go in.

Leaving the trug beside the shed, she returned to the house, tidied her overshoes onto the rack, pushed her feet into slippers. She was well practised and didn't make a sound. Along the passage upstairs, the wooden floors creaked randomly as the house warmed. No footsteps, not yet. She hung up her cardigan and made a pot of tea.

At the kitchen table, she ate a slice of white bread, thickly spread with butter like her father used to have with a wedge of cheese for his supper. From outside the dining room, the hall clock chimed the quarter-hour. At nine, she would serve the anniversary breakfast. Kippers, George wanted. Mrs James had bought them yesterday, and dusted everywhere, and ironed the best cloth. The anniversary gifts had been wrapped by the girls at Finningtons last week. 'A golden anniversary? Congratulations, madam. Goodness, that's worth a celebration, isn't it, sir?' The packages would be set on napkins at the table. She knew he had chosen pearls, large as the marbles the boys used to roll down the hall, oppressively white. She shuddered. But she would wear them, and he his cufflinks. Her woollen skirt and matching jacket were hanging on the padded mannequin in the dressing-room.

A noise above. She stood up, quickly as her joints allowed, wincing as the chair scraped on the old linoleum. The table must be laid, and the kippers poached, before he came downstairs.

Later, she sat stiff and still as the photographer fiddled with the sunshade. She listened vaguely to the clicking noises of the levers on his camera. She held a half-smile on her face and willed her shoulders not to shrink away from George, whose arm lay stretched along the back of the bench. His tweed jacket brushed her hip. He was a very physical man, leaving on every surface and in every moment an impression of himself. He'd insisted on laying the pearls around her neck, his fingers cold as he fumbled with the clasp. They were the wrong length. Too long to nestle above her collar, too short to sit smoothly on her chest. She thought of the seabed where they'd once hidden, shiny secrets trapped inside crusty shells.

She was uncomfortably aware of her bunions squeezed inside her shoes. Gleaming wine-red Oxfords with a stiff buckle that made the top of her feet bulge. The brown round-toed brogues would have been just as smart. Even these low heels were too much for her now. But he'd insisted. The red went with the thread in her skirt, he'd said. And now they wouldn't even be on show. He'd decided they would sit on the garden bench, their feet and his stick tucked out of sight.

Birdsong drifted from somewhere behind. She made out the sweet chirr of a robin. She and George had been still so long the little thing was probably darting up behind them, closer and closer, but she couldn't turn to look. George's wheezy breaths became heavier as he controlled his lack of patience. The smell of tobacco and tweed was so familiar she could, with a little effort, nose out the roses behind her. If she inhaled strongly, careful not to let her shoulders rise, the scent of some was distinct from others. The new golden hybrid that Cecil and Annie had brought her last week was the most recent addition, a pretty, single bloomer she knew would need training. Some of the roses were nearly as old as her marriage.

She had dug the beds with her father, the summer she and George moved in.

She shifted unobtrusively. Her left hip was beginning to hurt. The equipment still wasn't ready. She looked at the photographer, a youngish man, slim and fair. His hair flopped heavily onto his forehead as he bent over, left hand trembling as he made his adjustments. The silence was growing heavy. George never spoke to trade unless he had to.

'Do you have everything you need?' She tried to make her voice gentle but in her own ears she sounded quavery and cross. The photographer looked up.

'Oh yes, madam. Won't be a moment.' He smiled briefly.

'May I fetch you some water?' She would like to move. 'Or there's home-made lemonade? It's so hot – '

'Oh no, madam. Please stay where you are.' His voice was higher and more urgent than before, and she realised how silly she was being.

'Oh! Of course, I see.'

George tutted.

'Nearly there.' The photographer lifted his head a fraction and sent her another half-smile. 'Just tightening this.'

He twisted a lever into place and took a step back. The tripod lurched and the young man grabbed at it. On the back of the bench, behind her ear, she felt George's fist clench.

With the camera righted, the young man took a folded handkerchief from his trouser pocket and wiped his face. Mrs Brooker dropped her gaze to the arm of the old garden bench. The wood had been lightened by years of sun. It had stood on the patio opposite the French doors since – when was it? She couldn't remember exactly, but before the war. Her hand lay there, like something that didn't belong to her. The skin was livery, with veins standing up like ridges. She hadn't aged as handsomely as the chair.

'Are you ready?' She jumped. George was glaring at her. Pinkly, she nodded.

'Smile then, woman.'

'Thank you for coming in this evening, Mrs James,' said Mrs Brooker as the plates were cleared. 'The beef was delicious. Wasn't it, George?'

'What?' His head jerked up. 'Oh, yes. You did us proud.'

Mrs James nodded, pushing open the door with her bottom and disappearing towards the kitchen. George levered himself out of his chair.

'A *special* brandy, I think, don't you?' At the side table, he made a business of opening the tantalus and sliding out the decanters until he found what he was looking for. 'And one for you, dear?'

It was their routine, every anniversary and birthday. A small measure for him and a larger one for her. It was the sign. At least it meant no words had to be exchanged.

The table shone in the candlelight. The evening would soon be over. She sipped at the plummy, warm liquid, hoping it would do its job quickly.

'Were you pleased with how it went? The photograph?'

'Well, I don't know yet, do I?' He smeared a hand across his moustache. 'Ruddy well hope so, the price Melville is charging. Don't know why he didn't come himself. Chap he sent seemed a bit of a fairy to me.' He gulped at his drink. 'Did you see the way he quivered?'

'He was just a little nervous. Understandable, don't you think, in the circumstances?'

'What?'

'You are known about the town, dear. You were Councillor Brooker. Mayor Brooker.'

He corrected her. 'The Worshipful The Mayor. Yes, yes. I suppose that's true.' He smiled unpleasantly, showing the latest gap in his teeth. The lower set was a full denture. 'Chatted away to you afterwards though, didn't he, that chap?'

'Yes. Once he relaxed.' She'd insisted on refreshments, had fetched the jug and three glasses on a tray while the young man dismantled the equipment. George had fumbled on the ground for his stick and refused a drink. He'd gone stomping indoors to *The Times* while she poured sweet lemonade and Mr Finley sipped it gratefully and told her, reddening a little, about his failure to get into the army.

'He told me his wife is expecting any day.'

'Poor bastard.'

'He was charming.'

'Charming, eh?' His voice mimicked hers. 'Well, you've always been a fool for strange young men.'

Mrs Brooker looked down into her glass and swirled her brandy, until it rose perilously close to the rim.

They'd been married thirteen years and a day. That anniversary was lace, and he'd booked the overnight train to Bruges. Those were the times of George's grand gestures. He'd been promoted again and the boys were both away at school from Sunday night to Friday afternoon. He took her to bed as soon as they arrived at the hotel.

Afterwards, he went to rustle up some tea and she lay, half-propped on the bolster pillow and her breasts exposed, with the sheet tugged lazily to her waist. The sight would please him, when he came back. She was tired and sore, but happy, thinking of the days ahead when they would walk the lanes arm-in-arm. He'd promised a boat trip and a lace parasol and a full set of new tablecloths. Sunshine drifted through the heavy yellow drapes and burnished the thickly-painted walls, giving the room a lemony glow.

They argued over dinner though, when she realised they would not be home in time to see the boys that weekend.

'Of course we won't,' he said, tearing at his chicken with a rather blunt knife. 'We don't leave here 'til Sunday morning and there's a wait at Ostend for the boat. We'll be lucky to be back by midnight. My mother has agreed to have the boys and she'll get them off to school on time.' He chewed and swallowed. 'I told you all this.'

'You didn't, George. I only knew yesterday we were coming at all.' She speared a chunky piece of carrot and kept her voice light. 'Can we not go back a day earlier?'

'No, we cannot.' Gravy sprayed through his furious whisper. She glanced sidelong at the elderly couple at the next table. 'Good God, woman. Do you realise how long I've been planning this trip?'

She laid her fork on her plate and lifted her wine glass, put it down and poured water into their crystal tumblers. She focused on the dark middle of the candle flame and felt her eyes filling with tears.

'I don't want any fucking water,' he said. 'And you'll drink that fucking wine.'

It was still light when they emerged from the dining room, so she suggested a walk. Her head was swimming with the wine but her tears had retreated. She'd forced herself to eat and chat, thinking of the funny story she could tell the boys about the waiter who served them and his glass eye. They were still too young, she thought, to be sent away. At seven, Cecil was only just losing his baby teeth and his face changed shape, it seemed, every time she saw him. Albert was nearly twelve. Already, his arms hung grimly at his sides when she hugged him farewell. Soon he'd be at home only for holidays.

She took her husband's arm as they turned down Rue du Fil towards the canal. Her silk-covered Louis heels were unsteady on the cobbles and she steered him so that she could tread the smooth gully of the gutter.

'It was a lovely idea, George. Bringing us here.'

He patted her hand. The wine had softened his ire. 'Clever of me, wasn't it?' He leaned down to her ear. 'Now, just a short stroll and back to bed, eh?'

The narrow street was lined with a row of lace shops, closed for the night. She stopped at each, exclaiming over the fine designs and delicate work displayed in each window. As the sun dropped too low to reach between the tall buildings, she pointed upwards instead, at the equally intricate stair-step roofs and Gothic gables. George's pace relaxed and he sauntered with her, even stopping on a quaint bridge to admire a swan and her cygnets sailing through the dusk beneath.

They were circling back to the hotel when he said he needed to pee. He strode away into an alley, leaving her standing alone in the street. For a moment, the darkness was silent and complete. Then she heard a cough, a man announcing himself. She turned and he spoke in French, pointing in one direction and another. He was lost.

She smiled. *'Je suis desolé. Peut-être si vous parlez plus lentement–'*

When his hand clamped over her mouth she felt strangely unsurprised, as though the whole evening had been leading her to this moment. Her silk shoes scraped on the ground as she was dragged into a doorway, and quickly, horribly quickly, the man had his beery, wet mouth over hers and one hand up her skirts and inside her drawers, his fingers stubbing at her. She clawed and pressed at his hairy coat and tried to free her mouth to shout for George, for anyone, but the man was strong, tall and strong, and his other hand was around her neck, so tight she could not breathe.

When George yanked him away and sent him running off into the darkness, she sank to her haunches like an animal, her good bead purse clattering to the stones, her gloved hands cradling her neck. She wanted to vomit and spit out the stranger's foul breath. She wanted to hide away in that doorway forever. George gathered her to her feet, and supported her all the way back to their room, shielding her from the concerned but curious gaze of the concierge. And in the room, he undressed her, gently tugging off each shoe, patiently undoing each tiny button of her dress. He lifted her in his arms and laid her in the bed and got in next to her and stroked her head.

But then, in the middle of the night, she woke to find him on top of her, groping at one breast, groaning as he pushed his way inside. She stared upwards, over his heaving shoulder, to the ceiling where the moon threw a hazy bar of light across one corner of the room.

She and George went up the staircase together like newly-weds, hand-in-hand. He used his stick and she carried the dregs of her brandy and they both had to pause at the top to catch their breath. The smell of roast beef and cabbage lingered. In his room, she helped him take off his jacket and as he dropped his trousers, she placed a cushion on the floor for her knees.

When he sat on the edge of the bed, his excitement was already clear. She swigged back the last of her drink. He gripped her head so hard she knew it would hurt for days. When it was over, mercifully quickly, she spat the tiny salty spoonful of his seed into her empty tumbler and pressed her lips to the sleeve of her blouse. She placed her hands on his old white knees to help herself up. 'Goodnight, George,' she said. 'Happy anniversary, dear.'

It rained overnight. She flung the kitchen window wide, letting in the scent of the jasmine and nicotiana as she boiled the kettle and made up a tray for George. A plate of thinly cut toast, no butter, a small dish of bramble jelly and a spoon.

She set the cosy over the teapot and his cup on its saucer and poured in a drop of milk.

The unwashed brandy glass sat beside the sink. She touched two fingers to a tender place above her ear. Taking a firm grip on the tray, she trod carefully into the hall and up the stairs. In George's room, she drew back the curtains partway. He didn't stir. His thick white hair was mussed against the pillow, his snores gentle. She stood in the half-light and watched his chest move up and down.

She went all the way down the garden path in her robe. Yesterday's dead-headed roses lay wilting in their trug. She lifted her hem over the puddle that had formed at the door of the greenhouse. It was already sultry inside. The tomatoes breathed with her and the thought of her father and his green-stained fingers filled her mind as she gathered a half-dozen ripe fruit into her pockets. They would go with the cold beef for lunch.

Jane's first job was in her local library, and these days she makes a living advising schools and teachers on books and teaching English. She is mum to two teenagers and three cats, and lives in the South Downs. She has published numerous textbooks and study guides and her fiction experience includes the Creative Writing Programme and Advanced Writing Workshops at New Writing South in Brighton. Jane's writing tends to explore family dynamics and relationships. She is on Instagram:

@janebranson and can also be contacted through her website: www.janebransonlearning.co.uk.

Requiem For A Woolwich Canary

by Sarah Doyle

'...for some, the effects of their work were immediately visible; a lurid shade of yellow that stained their skin and hair and earned them a nickname: the Canary Girls.'

http://www.bbc.co.uk/news/uk-england-39434504

> These women are doing their bit. Learn to make munitions.
>
> *Ministry of Munitions recruitment poster, circa 1915*

'Doin' their bit? Fallin' to bits, more like!'

The mouth that squawked the joke had very few teeth in it and was a vivid slash of scarlet against a jowly and slightly jaundiced face. It belonged to the largest woman I'd ever seen. Certainly the loudest I'd ever met. The fabric of her brown overall strained across an enormous bosom that heaved with laughter. 'Doin' their bit!' she repeated, clearly delighted. 'Where are you from? Under the mulberry bush?'

'No, Esher. And this is my first visit to Woolwich'. She howled with mirth and immediately I regretted my embarrassingly straight answer. Flustered now, I tried again. 'You see, the poster, last year, in the Guildhall, it said that we should all do our bit and I've been waiting until I turned eighteen –'

'And very noble you are, too, angel. Now if you'd just like to pop your halo and wings in the staffroom –'

She was interrupted by the approach of a tall, straight-backed woman in spectacles. 'Thank you, Violet. I was un-aware that your duties had been extended to include the reception of new recruits. Perhaps you would kindly return to the line, I'm sure your particular brand of morale-maintenance is being missed. And wear your hairnet!'

The woman called Violet winked at me, cast a stage-whispered 'See you later, angel!' out of the side of her crimson lips and waddled off in the direction of a distant tinny clatter, muttering 'Who ruffled her feathers, then?' all the while.

I tried to regain some ground. 'Hello, you must be Agatha, I'm –'

'Yes, I know who you are. And I –' she bristled a little – 'am Miss Thewell. Follow me, please. We need to get you into overalls, gloves, net and so forth. You have lodgings?'

She started walking and I scurried to keep pace.

'Yes, thank you. I'm at Mrs Wattle's. A large room, at the top of the house, quite comfy, with two windows, and only one other girl sharing the bathroom –'

My enthusiasm for my lodgings was genuine. I had

expected dark walls and stark austerity, but my new rented bedroom was papered with a cheery mix of flowers and birds, the two windows of my attic eyrie affording far-reaching views of rooftops, chimney-stacks and the welcome water-colour green of distant trees.

I would have told Miss Thewell all of this, too, if mercifully she hadn't silenced me with a curt nod as we entered what I took to be a staffroom-cum-changing room. Battered but serviceable armchairs lined three walls, while a fourth was dominated by a rail of outdoor coats at one end and overalls at the other. A rimed kettle perched on a two-ring gas hob next to a large butler sink in one corner.

'Yes, yes, Mrs Wattle keeps a respectable house. You will wear these.' She held out a long brown coat, the smaller sister of the one that Violet had been wearing. 'And a hairnet. Boots, mask. Gloves, no jewellery. No cigarettes or matches to be about your person. One tea-break per shift, as per the rota. When you're changed, please come to the floor and ask for Daphne. She'll show you the ropes, and talk to you about safety precautions. You'll be on mortar shells, with relatively light duties for a day or two, until we see what you're made of –'

'I hope of sound moral fibre,' I interrupted her, still eager to make good my apparent faux pas in associating myself with Violet.

She arched an owlish eyebrow. 'Quite. Hurry along now.'

Her heels clicked a staccato exit across the tiled floor.

'I take it you've met Naggy Aggy, then?'

Daphne was as thin as Violet had been fat but her sharp features were softened by a crinkle around her eyes and a surprising, generous smile that transformed her sallow face.

'Oh, Miss Thewell, yes –' I tried not to betray my shock at such blatant insubordination.

Daphne was quick to respond. 'Don't worry about Naggy Aggy, love. She knows what we call her. Just don't let her hear you doing it. Come on, I'll take you over.'

She led me across the factory's vast floor, navigating rows of workbenches peopled by hundreds of women, through the confused din of voices and machines, the mingled smells of sweat and metal and something more pungent – perhaps oniony, I thought. It was a cathedral of a place, heads bent over benches and bomb-parts in a parody of prayer. And it was freezing.

'Why is it so cold?' The question had left my lips before I'd had a chance to bite it back. I knew that I must have sounded silly, and was embarrassed by it, but really, my arms were covered in quivering goose-bumps, even beneath the thick fabric of my overall sleeves.

Daphne stopped and looked at me. 'Have you ever worked with explosives before?' I shook my head. 'Well, try heating the place up and see what'd happen.' Seeing my mortified look, she gave me that smile again. 'Don't worry, I'll take you under my wing. Come and meet the girls.'

Violet I recognised, of course. In addition, I was introduced to Joan, Mags, Reenie and Queenie (spinster twins of indeterminate middle age) and sundry other women whose names and faces blurred before me. This was my first foray into the world of work – into the world at large, come to that – and I felt shy, overwhelmed and giddy. Again, Daphne read me with hawkish intuition. 'You'll soon get to know us all, you'll see. And you'll settle right in, I'm sure. Just eighteen, ain't you?'

I nodded. 'Yes. Not much older than the century, my father always says.'

'Not much of a century it's turning out to be!' came Violet's shrill call from the other side of a work bench. 'Bombs, bullets and getting blown to buggery!'

'Violet!' Daphne was laughing in spite of herself. 'Having a soldier for a son doesn't mean you can talk like one.'

Violet laughed her booming guffaw. 'Stop clucking round the new girl, Daph, she ain't made of china. She'll go from green to yellow soon enough.'

Daphne shook her head indulgently, calling out a good-natured 'Just you mind your own business, Missus Sticky-Beak!' before taking me gently by the arm. 'Come on, love,' she said, 'I'll take you through what's what.'

With Daphne's patience and the ready help of my new colleagues, I started to settle in and to feel more confident with each passing day and week. Although the work was physically demanding, not to say unpleasant – dirty, fiddly, smelly – I loved it, taking to factory life like the old duck to water. I was on shell assembly, tamping waxy phosphorus into the glitter of cordite within surprisingly delicate metal casings, before inserting the stiff strand of a fuse: a yolk for every egg. I had been terrified of the materials at first, flinching at my every own movement, but familiarity and pragmatism soon replaced my initial wariness. Sometimes, I couldn't help but worry about ending up like Vi and some of the rest of them – thinning hair, lost teeth, and the other-worldly dull gold of their skin and hair. But when I thought of the horrors and hardships being suffered by our soldiers in France or Belgium, my resolve was always bolstered.

I'd never felt useful before and certainly had never had any money in my purse – at least not my own earned money. I had also never experienced such company. I remembered very little of my mother, having been so young when she'd died, but the memories I had were of a softly-spoken reserve and a brittle femininity. Similarly, the girls I had known during my sheltered schooling had been from comfortable backgrounds like mine and, like me, they had been versed in politeness and constraint. The language used by the women at Woolwich would have curled every hair on my quiet, academic father's head. And yet, after a while, my shock subsided into acceptance and even pleasure at hearing the chirpy factory banter – although I drew the line at joining in with Violet's improvised choruses of 'It's the wrong day to lick a Mary'.

I learned that Violet was cheerfully widowed, the mother of two sons, Percy and Dickie. Percy was away, fighting, and she couldn't have been prouder of him, keeping her anxiety for his welfare well-hidden beneath frequent jokes about the Kaiser, combined with stinging criticisms of what little she knew about British military strategy. Her older son, Dickie, lived at home with her. He was what Daphne described to me privately as simple, although Violet herself would have no truck with the word. 'He's a special one, is my Dickie,' she would proclaim, at least once a day. 'A good boy. A true comfort.'

Reenie and Queenie were identical, lived together and spoke in unison, too. Both had missing fingers, although I never liked to look closely to see if these injuries were also identical. The twins were friendly in a self-contained kind of a way, although I was often disconcerted by their dual voices and the way their bright, darting eyes always seemed to be conveying some secret or other.

Joan had four adult daughters, all married and all 'doing their bit', working in different munitions factories nearer their own homes. All had been married to men who'd enlisted. Two were widowed.

Mags was also married, and fairly recently from what I could make out. Her husband was a corporal, fighting in France, and she carried his photograph with her everywhere she went, tucked inside the left cup of her brassiere – next to her heart, she said. She claimed not to have slept a wink since he'd gone, and although I suspected that this could not actually be true, I sympathised with her fretfulness and included her Alf every night in my bedtime prayers.

Months passed. Although I'd be exhausted each night and fall into bed gratefully, I had begun to feel frequently bilious, and found that my own sleep – once easily come by, and with very few dreams – had become increasingly erratic since starting at Woolwich, and was populated by progressively vivid and confusing images. Mags's Alf, Violet's Percy, Joan's surviving sons-in-law and countless other faceless men all flickered across my night-time landscape in distorted whorls of flying mud, accompanied by the chaotic cacophony of male screams, shell blasts, horses' terrified whinnies. Night after night, I would lurch into queasy wakefulness, burning up yet still shivering, blinking my eyes free of the ghastly visions before slumping back onto my sweat-soaked pillow. My teeth ached and my scalp prickled. I didn't speak to any of the other girls about my night-terrors, not wanting to appear weak or highly-strung.

It was with gratitude mingled, if I'm honest, with a little trepidation, that I accepted an invitation to Sunday tea at Violet's house. I had grown to like her enormously, her constant fund of chit-chat and dirty songs having helped us all to keep our peckers up throughout the long shifts, but I wasn't sure that we would have a great deal to talk about when it was just the two of us. That said, I felt that I'd had a great honour conferred upon me with such an unexpected and kind invitation, and wouldn't have dreamed of giving offence with a refusal.

Violet's front-door was a well-kept lacquered affair, its glossy black finish and gleaming brass knocker somewhat incongruous in the greying expanse of an unevenly cobbled street. The watery Woolwich sunshine showed where my fingers left small, dull smudges on the yellow metal.

I'd barely finished my tentative knock when the door was opened a crack and the large, moonlike face of a man peered at me with suspicious curiosity through the narrow space. I mustered a smile and spoke with artificial breeziness.

'Hello. You must be Dickie. Is your mother here? I've come for tea.'

He closed the door abruptly and I could hear his heavy footsteps retreating into the house, his slightly slurred voice calling, 'Mum, Mum, she's here, lady's here, lady's on the step, Mum –'

I heard the distant flush of an outhouse, followed by Violet's unmistakable tones.

'Well, don't leave her there, Dickie. Fetch her in. Go on. Like you wanted to. Like we practised.'

A few seconds passed and the door was opened again, fully this time, to reveal a tall, rangy man sporting freshly-oiled hair, knee-length trousers and what was, without doubt, his best shirt and pullover, the whole ensemble finished with a lopsided bowtie. He smiled shyly but determinedly and made an elaborate gesture of welcome with his hands.

His pronouncement was touchingly well-rehearsed. 'Please do come in,' he intoned, solemnly. 'We are glad to make your acquaintance.'

My smile was genuine this time. 'Thank you. And glad to make your acquaintance, I'm sure.' I struggled out of my coat, which he placed with care on the bottom banister.

Violet emerged, occupying her narrow hallway's entire width. 'Yes, yes, you're glad, he's glad, we're all glad, even the King's glad, I'll wager. Now fetch yourself in, angel, for Gawd's sake, and we can all have a bite of tea.'

She ushered me into the front parlour, where a table had been set for three. Dickie rushed to pull back my chair for me and laid a napkin solicitously on my lap, while Violet brought in a cosied teapot. I was peckish for once, and didn't need telling twice to tuck into the sandwiches of potted meat. 'Crusts cut off, they are,' Dickie informed me through a half-chewed mouthful. 'Like posh.'

Violet laughed with a softness and affection I'd never witnessed in the factory. 'He insisted,' she said. 'Been talking about this all week. Ain't you?'

Dickie blushed and rolled his eyes, then resumed his surreptitious appraisal of me, whilst nursing a succession of further sandwiches. I was relieved to find that Violet and I chatted quite easily, with me telling her about my father, our house, the dogs, my old school; and her sharing reminiscences of childhood, courtship, the boys' longdead father. We ate home-made scones ('Dickie helped, didn't you?') and drank more tea. An hour passed comfortably, although Dickie was becoming increasingly agitated, trying to catch his mother's attention, rolling his eyes in the direction of the parlour door. Eventually, Violet laughed. 'Oh, go on then, I know you've been dying to show her.'

Dickie dismounted his chair and shot out of the room like a cannonball, careering off the doorframe as he went. I heard his footsteps pounding the stairs. There was a brief hiatus before he crashed back down, entering the room at a skid, something clearly clutched behind his back. At this, his resolve seemed to leave him a little, and he looked to his mother for reassurance. Violet's voice was all tenderness. 'Go on, you wanted to show them to her. She'd like to see them.' She turned to me: 'Wouldn't you?'

I answered in the affirmative, with what I hoped were

encouraging tones, despite not knowing the contents of Dickie's hands. Slowly, like a half-wild thing newly-tamed, Dickie approached me. He brought out from behind his back a large, battered biscuit tin with a faded picture of the king on its lid. His voice was tentative, but clear. 'My c'llection. I wanted to show you.'

With a nod of consent from Violet, I prised open the lid, folding it back on rusting hinges. Inside the tin lay an assortment of feathers, ranging from the workaday greys of pigeons to the warmer brown tones of pheasants, and all peppered with the occasional blue flash of a magpie's garb. But what caught my attention was the large white feather that curled round on itself several times, clinging to the tin's perimeter like an exotically fronded snake. Compulsively, I reached out a hand to it. It was so soft, my fingertips could hardly register it.

All this time, Dickie's eyes had been fixed on me, a look of pride and wonder on his face. 'I find them,' he told me, earnestly. 'I don't hurt the birds. I keep what they don't want.'

Violet's voice was almost reverential. 'Walks all the way to Falconwood Field for 'em, don't you, Dickie? Sits dead still for hours, he does, just watching the birds, hoping for a feather.'

I smiled, still stroking the white feather. 'They're lovely,' I said, and meant it. 'But what about this one, Dickie? There can't be many ostriches in England.'

His face split into a grin and the eyes rolled again. 'That was Percy. He sent me it. From France. From a lady.'

I looked at Violet for an explanation. 'It's true,' she said. 'Percy and his lot had a couple of nights' stopover in Lille on their way through. He sent Dickie this feather and a note, all about how it belonged to a showgirl he'd met, but whether or not that's true...' She shrugged. 'He always was one for stories. Lawd knows what he got up to, a mother doesn't like to think.' Her tone became pinched. 'I just hope he's alright, wherever he is now.'

Without even looking, she reached a hand behind her, where she sought and found a framed photograph, one of a forest of them on the mantelpiece, and passed it to me. Percy's face was strong, angular. His eyes were direct and clear, just a hint of a smile playing about full lips beneath a toothbrush moustache. Photographed from the shoulders up, he was in cap and uniform, any trepidation buried beneath a discernible layer of defiance and pride. I was surprised to find my heart beating faster and hastily handed back the picture, trying to hide my stupid girlish blushes by manufacturing renewed interest in Dickie's feathers. Not long after, I made my excuses, offered my thanks for a lovely afternoon, and left.

Although tired, I couldn't bring myself to lie down that night, instead dragging a chair to the larger of my windows and perching on it, for hours perhaps, adrift in thought. My eyes took in the nightscape: the thinning curls of pale chimney smoke against the dark sky, the indiscernible smudges of tree canopies, the smear of stars. But my gaze was unfocused, distant, as I imagined what lay beyond my view: the terracotta terraces of south London, the fields of Kent, the English Channel, Lille, France. Battlefields.

I closed my eyes and pictured a French showgirl, hitching up her skirts and high-kicking her legs in time to raucous accordion music, accompanied by the approving roar of soldiers – of Percy. I imagined his face: the full, nearly-smiling lips, kissing her, kissing me, whispering promises that would inevitably be broken.

I must have dozed off, because I jerked awake as I slipped sideways, almost falling off my seat. I was chilled to the bone. Too late for a fire, I pulled on my outdoor coat for instant warmth and slid into bed, hunkering down beneath my bed-covers, hands deep in my coat-pockets. I was almost asleep before the fingers of my right hand registered something alien. I extracted the article and held it up. It was a raven's feather, no doubt one of Dickie's collection, which he must have secreted in my unattended coat pocket. A souvenir of the day.

I fell asleep holding it, to dream of soldiers and show-girls, mud and music, and of a sky raining with sharp black feathers.

1916 became 1917. I spent a muted but contented New Year's Eve at home with my father, glad of a respite from the rigours of Woolwich and from Dickie's attentions. He had taken to leaving little tokens for me on my landlady's doorstep. An old wren's egg; a dry, curling fern tied with ribbon; even a dead sparrow, frost-rimed and stiff as sticks.

The winter was harsh, bitterly cold and long-lasting. We would arrive for our shifts already frozen to the marrow, feet and hair damp with slush or sleet; and we'd stay that way throughout the day in the well-ventilated cavern of the factory. I was a walking ghost, pale and insubstantial as London snow, never sleeping properly, but never fully awake, either. Even the onset of a feeble Spring and the subtle change in the gifts that Dickie left me – withered bluebells, unidentifiable mushrooms – failed to penetrate the fug that seemed to surround me, like smoke.

When I did sleep, I'd dream frequently of Percy, although in my dreams he was often an amalgam of the characteristics of others, my unconscious imagination filling in the gaps as it saw fit. He was variously English or French; he would wear an army uniform with short trousers and a bowtie; he sat in my father's chair and read me stories about showgirls; he was standing still as a statue on the blood-drenched mud of a battlefield, draped in sinuous white feathers, an arm stretched out to me, an arm that I couldn't quite reach, no matter how desperately I tried...

The morning after a particularly disturbed night dawned with a grey, half-hearted drizzle and I made my way unsteadily to the factory with face bent low over my chest, my scarf pulled tightly about my head and neck, already exhausted before the day had begun. I knew something was wrong as soon I entered the staffroom to change. Mags, Reenie and Queenie, Daph, Joan – even Naggy Aggy – were all sitting on the tattered armchairs in an atmosphere of thick, soupy silence. The kettle started to whine its readiness and Joan obeyed its summons as if in a daze, busying herself with cups and sixteen spoons. I perched on the arm of a chair. 'What is it?' I asked. I scanned the room. 'Where's Vi?'

Daph spoke in a flat monotone, not meeting my eye. 'She's had the letter. A telegram. Her Percy.'

My heart pulsed tightly in my throat. I swallowed. 'Missing?' I didn't dare hope. Daph shook her head.

'Gone. Killed in action. They won't even tell her where. She don't even know if there'll be anything to bury'.

'Oh, poor Vi...' It was all I could muster although my mind was flying and I wanted to say so much more. I wondered if she'd held the letter in her hands a long time before opening it, not wanting to know its awful contents, or if she'd torn at it desperately, needing to get it over with, to face it head on. Did Dickie know? Would he understand, even if he did? Poor Vi, I thought again. It would be just her now; just her, and her sweet, simple son, and no-one to look after her if she gets old – only worry and loneliness and loss. Fury and pity eddied around inside me until I felt myself sway a little on my perch.

'Drink this. It's nice and sweet. We all need one.' Joan forced a hot cup into my hands. Naggy Aggy stood and smoothed her hair with fluttering fingers.

'Five minutes, girls. Then back to the grindstone.' Her voice had lost all its crispness and bluster, and I found myself longing for yesterday when everything was normal and Vi had had two sons and Naggy Aggy hadn't seemed human.

The day dragged like no other. Out on the floor, we girls barely spoke as we worked, each of us locked in our own private worlds, and no-one wanting to break the spell of hush that settled on our corner of the factory. With the surgical deftness I had come to perfect, I placed another finished shell in the soft straw of its pallet. It nestled there innocently, like a chick in its nest. Absently I traced my initials onto the smooth metal of its body. My gloved finger left no mark, so I moistened it with my tongue and drew my initials again. This time, the snake of the letters glistened wetly and I experienced a satisfied thrill, thinking that when it exploded in some German trench I would be there, too, a part of it. Doing my bit. I wondered if there would be a German version of Vi, weeping bitterly for a lost son in Hamburg or Berlin or wherever, and I hoped that there was. I hoped there were hundreds, thousands of them, weeping for lost sons, lost sweethearts, lost hope. My initials, though dried, were still discernible on the shell's casing when I closed the crate at the end of my shift. A part of me, going into war.

That night, my dreams were stranger than ever, yet much clearer, too. I dreamt that my fingers were receding, my arms tapering to wings, while the heavy, aching clubs of my bones contracted, thinning into fine, porcelain reeds. I was flying, though where I didn't know. France, perhaps? Belgium? I was aware of a new-found resolve and a metallic determination pulsing through my veins. Phosphorus lay expectantly in my gut, ready to drop with me. I couldn't tell if I was a bird or a bomb.

The face regarding me in my bedroom mirror the following morning was tinged with a sickly lunar patina; but, though disoriented, I was filled with a clarity of purpose completely unfamiliar to me.

At the factory, I barely spoke to the other girls, just nodding a curt greeting before applying myself to my work.

Surreptitiously, at intervals throughout the day, I slipped off a glove and bit through one of my fingernails until I had a jagged half-moon between my lips. Everyone was still so cut up about Vi, no-one was looking at me. It was easy to slip a fragment of fingernail, a tiny talisman, into a shell along with its legitimate explosive contents. At the end of my shift I left the factory, satisfied in the knowledge that ten Woolwich shells would be taking a miniscule part of me into battle with them. Ten talons, ready to claw out the eyes of any number of German soldiers. I slept well that night, for the first time in months.

Of course, the nightmares soon returned: the strangled screams of dying men, the stench of blood and faeces. The smoky, choking air. Exhaustion and dizziness had become the natural order for me, to such a degree that I hardly noticed them, simply accepting the heavy ache in my limbs and joints.

I had a couple of back-teeth that had started to come loose and which I would jiggle with my tongue or a finger at every opportunity. It took several weeks but I finally wrested them free of my bleeding gums, wrapping them carefully in a hankie to take to the factory. The girls had become accustomed to my withdrawn conduct and took little notice of me. Even Vi, who was back at work now, barely looked up when she saw me.

I worked diligently, as always. Twice through the morning, I opened my hankie and retrieved one of my twin treasures, embedding it in the pungent phosphorus before tamping the potent mix into its shell. I would tear at the enemy's flesh with my teeth, I thought. And I wouldn't stop until they were shreds. With a giddy satisfaction, I carried the second of my adapted shells to the crate –

and stumbled.

My eyes were so unfocused, I hardly had time to register the smooth metal ovoid slipping out of my limp hands and arcing gracefully towards the floor.

Distant voices insinuated themselves at the edge of my consciousness.

'Quick, Doctor, I think she's waking up!' – Naggy Aggy?

Then an unfamiliar male voice: 'I don't think so, Miss Thewell. She's slipping –'

The voices faded to nothing, as if whipped away by fast-moving fog. I was dimly aware of a prone figure but the image had been so fleeting that I couldn't retain it on my fast-flickering retinas. My world was metamorphosing, my mind a map, every synapse and fibre a burgeoning fund of geography.

My belly and breasts smoothed into one continuous aerodynamic curve, my legs shrinking to spindles and folding perfectly into the feathered undercarriage of my almost weightless body, my arms taking on the familiar fan-shape of wings. My small, pointed tongue sought out and loosened any remaining teeth as my lips hardened, elongating into a beak.

From somewhere – from everywhere, from around me, from inside me – I heard the high, trilling song of a canary and knew that the voice was mine. Before the darkness came, I filled my tiny lungs with sky, to sing my name, again and again and again: Ava.

Sarah Doyle is the Pre-Raphaelite Society's Poet-in-Residence. She has been published widely in journals and anthologies, and placed in numerous competitions, being the winner of several. She was highly commended in the Forward Prizes 2018 and is published in *Poems of the Decade: An Anthology of the Forward Books of Poetry 2011-2020*. Sarah holds an MA in Creative Writing from UL Royal Holloway, and is currently researching a PhD in meteorological poetry at Birmingham City University. A pamphlet of poems collaged from fragments of Dorothy Wordsworth's journals – *Something so wild and new in this feeling* – was published by V. Press in 2021.

Website: www.sarahdoyle.co.uk

Twitter: @PoetSarahDoyle

A Place in the Sun

'For God's sake woman, tie the bloody screwdriver in.'

As Anne Crawford looked up, shielding her eyes from the sun, she could only make out her husband's backside around the edges of the bosun's chair and the peak of his skipper's cap.

'Into what?' she shouted.

'The line,' he bellowed back.

'The line?'

'In front of you. There! Christ alive!'

The line hung in the shadow her husband and his chair cast on the deck. As Anne took hold of it, she thought of Rachel and The Blue Mosque.

'It's just a boy's adventure for him, as usual,' her daughter had sighed. 'Why are you even going, Mum? And with your hip. Why don't you come to Istanbul with us?'

Jerry often spent weekends sailing near home, but he liked 'at least one adventure a year on the high seas.' She'd hoped there might be other holidays, now that he worked less, but when she'd mentioned this to him, minus any reference to

Rachel of course, it had only triggered a tirade. 'No sense of adventure... no spirit... bloody typical of you,' before he screeched off in his Porsche to the sailing club.

As she watched him pull the screwdriver back up the mast, Anne leaned against the port side of *The Bonus*. How many times had she heard him at the club, 'Hah! Why *The Bonus*? Because it was paid for by one. A bloody big one!'

She rubbed her hip, making an effort to stand up straight, and looked out over the endless miles of the Atlantic.

Jerry had swum in the sea on their first date, fifty-two years ago. He'd only passed his driving test the day before and she remembered the journey down to Brighton, with him telling her stories and playing the fool, asking what she thought about all manner of things, things that were never discussed on trips with her parents.

As soon as they parked, he was off, running down the beach, scrambling into his trunks behind a towel. He leaped into the sea, calling her as she looked for somewhere to change.

'Come on, Annie girl! What's the matter with you?'

She couldn't tell him she'd never been in the sea before, that her parents weren't the sort to go to the seaside. Swimming had only ever meant paint-box blue chlorinated water at the local pool.

By the time she was standing up to her waist in the water, shivering, he had reached the bright orange buoy. He turned around and waved at her, smiling wildly. She'd waved back, smiling too, despite the cold. She pushed out a little towards him, straining her neck to keep her face out of the water, before turning back into the safety of the shallows. Then he was with her, lifting her up into the air, wrapping his arms around her back and legs. She felt the strength in his arms and she didn't feel cold anymore; she felt light and alive.

On their return, he swept into the parking space outside her parents' house like a visiting film star. Her mother watched them arrive from behind the net curtains. He escorted Anne, through the gate and for the few steps to the front door, his hand in the small of her back, before knocking loudly on the door. He shook her father's hand and complimented her mother on the beautiful house. Her mother offered them a jug of squash and a plate of biscuits and Anne watched him standing in front of the old dresser, tingling with energy after a day in the sun, and she knew that the room, the terraced house, the street were all too small for him. She decided at that moment that she wanted to be with him, in a place that was big enough, wherever that was.

She pulled the cover-up around her. Her hip was aching this morning. The surgeon had warned her that she would have to work through some pain for the first few months. She'd told Jerry before they left that she was worried about doing any of the physical work on the trip.

'You're on light duties, Anne. Cooking, cleaning, making the drinks. You my Girl Friday. I'll do the rest.'

It never helped when she didn't sleep well, and she rarely slept well when Jerry snored. At home, she would move to the spare room, but here she stayed in the bed, not wanting to walk around the moving boat in the dark. So, she lay next to his snorts and gasps, watching his spittle dribble down his chin. Asleep, he looked just like his father after she'd cooked them Sunday dinner.

'Lovely grub,' his dad would say as he slumped into the chair. 'He's a lucky boy, my Jerry. It wasn't easy for him you know, without his mum, but he's got you now.' Then the same line every week. 'And so, good lady, it's time for some Egyptian PT.' He would be snoring even before she'd cleared the table.

She looked up at Jerry, fifty or sixty feet above her, whistling *A Sailor's Life for Me* into the vast sky.

'Where are all the birds?' she'd asked earlier, looking through the binoculars he kept hooked inside the flybridge.

'Birds! Those binoculars are for looking at boats, woman. Birds aren't going to be out here, are they? This far from the shore. God Almighty! How's your geography? Besides, who wants seagulls? They're a bloody pest.' He shook his head. 'Right, I'm going up to sort out the weather electronics. Captain's responsibility.'

She'd watched as the remote-controlled winch took him up on to the bosun's chair. She could see his delight as his newest piece of kit transported him upwards.

'I'll hook myself on at the top,' he shouted halfway up, waving a large stainless steel clip at her, 'I don't want you wiping me off the deck just yet,' he snorted.

The boat, and all its paraphernalia, was impressive. It didn't surprise her. The equipment Jerry bought was always impressive.

'It's a magnificent vessel, *The Bonus,* and Sir Jeremy's a first class skipper,' David had told her at the Sailing Club bar, 'but it's a risky business, if I may say so, Tenerife to Antigua with just the two of you. No disrespect to you, Lady Crawford, but it's really a job for at least two able seamen. We'll be doing the trip just in front of you, and it'll be me and Sandy, plus Roger and Deborah. So, two able seamen, plus, two Prosecco experts,' he guffawed.

When she'd mentioned this to Jerry, he scoffed, 'Hah! I'll enjoy seeing his face when we sail into the harbour at Antigua. You watch. It'll be bloody priceless.'

He'd spent the first morning talking her through the 'aboard ship' rules and equipment, as he did every trip. She nodded automatically as he spoke. Although she had learnt about the 'radars' and 'satellites' when he first got the boat, she knew Jerry would take care of all that stuff once they were at sea. He did the boat, she did the food.

With Jerry busy at the top of the mast, Anne opened her cover-up and looked down at her new bikini. She wouldn't normally wear one, but she enjoyed the sun and no one would have to see her out here at sea. She would just stand on deck for a bit, to see how the bikini felt. To feel the sun on her skin. She took the cover-up off.

A moment later she heard him.

'Christ. Put it away, woman!'

She looked up at him, shielding her eyes from the sun. He was leaning away from the rigging, looming above her.

'A woman of your age in that? No, really. If I'd have wanted that, I'd have brought somebody else,' he snorted.

She reached for the cover-up and wrapped it around herself.

Jerry always said, 'Men grow into their looks. Women wither,' but was it silly to wear a bikini at her age? She looked at herself through his eyes and saw the long scar on her hip, the wrinkled skin across her knees and the liver spots on her shins that seemed to have multiplied since she last looked. She ran her finger down the scar. It was smooth and not unpleasant to touch. Without looking back up at her husband, she took the steps down to the cabin, always leading with her strong leg, and into the berth to change.

It wasn't easy with him being around more. All their married life, Jerry had split his time between the offices in London and Geneva. 'The Swiss are the financial law experts,' he told her. By the time his sole partner died, ACC Group had over two hundred staff, with an additional office in Vaduz, all, 'facilitating a global pathway to minimise our clients' tax liabilities.'

He was away from home even more once he became CEO. 'The Swiss need me there,' he told her. And then came the new office in St Vincent, with additional business to oversee.

When he was home, he was more and more at The Carlton Club, 'Having dinner with Ken, who assured me... really productive meeting with Michael, who thinks we can do something mutually beneficial...' She met him there for lunch once. They ate in the Members' Dining Room, surrounded by portraits of Tory grandees.

'Don't wear trousers,' he told her. 'Remember, women weren't PLU here, until recently.'

'PLU?'

'People like us.'

They held the reception at the Carlton after he received his Knighthood. 'For services to British commerce.' The London office organised it but there were representatives from the other centres too. The women from the Swiss office in particular, smiling and immaculate, speaking perfect English, made her feel old and slightly dowdy, despite the dress she'd taken so long to choose. Jerry left her with a group from the London office, whose wives told her how proud she must be, before discussing the price of houses. Their husbands drifted over from time to time, to impress upon her what a privilege it was to work for the company under Sir Jeremy's leadership, before making their excuses and moving back to their colleagues. As she listened to them talk about golf, she watched Jerry being guided around the room by his elegant Executive Assistant.

After dinner, an assured young woman from the extended Leadership Group stood up and announced, 'Our leader, Sir Jeremy Crawford.' The whole room stood in appreciation, applauding loudly, whilst Jerry motioned with his hands for them to sit down. Listening, she realised that all of Jerry's conversations these days sounded like speeches.

She sometimes wondered if the Jerry she'd known was still in there at all.

She changed into a pair of three-quarter length, linen trousers to cover the liver spots, along with sandals and a loose, long-sleeved top. As she headed to the steps, she saw Jerry's copy of *The Telegraph* on the table. The crossword was unfinished. After the knighthood, he had begun to have fairly frequent coverage in the press. One article in *The Telegraph* had called him, 'The rich and powerful's Mr Fix It.' An unnamed source had said, 'There doesn't seem to be a problem he can't solve.' He'd hung a framed copy of the article in their downstairs loo.

She looked up at Jerry. He was leaning over to the right in the bosun's seat, away from the mast and swaying gently. She shielded her eyes and squinted. He was still clipped in, but his torso, neck and head were lolling over the side of the seat. His skipper's cap hung precariously at an angle.

'Jerry?'

She heard her voice. Slightly reedy.

'Jerry!' she called more strongly.

His skipper's cap fell, landing at her feet on the deck. She stared at it then looked up, waiting for him to move, expecting him to spring to life and shout, 'Don't just stand there, woman, pick it up!' But he didn't. The seat had stopped swaying and now simply hung above her. She called up to him again, sharply now. But he didn't reply. She took the binoculars off their hook.

'Jerry?'

The lens was filled with the blue of his shirt. She adjusted the focus, and could see the right-hand side of his face and forehead. His eye was open, unblinking, staring ahead. His mouth was open too. If his eyes had been shut, he could have been snoring in his sleep. She held the binoculars steady, looking for any breathing movement, or flicker of life. There was only his shirt, billowing in the breeze.

She sat down on the bench behind the flybridge. 'Oh,' she murmured. She counted to twenty, before looking up again, steadying the binoculars. He still hung in the same position.

'Oh, Jerry.'

She closed her eyes.

When Valerie's Brian died earlier that year, she'd had the words. 'Such a shock… sincere condolences… deepest sympathy…' now they merged with the splash and lap of the water, the clicking of the rigging, the flap of the canvas and slipped away. She felt the heat of the sun on her eyelids and opened her eyes.

'Jerry?' She called up again.

'Jerry?' she shouted.

She would need to tell Rachel. She wondered if she would cry.

The controller for the winch was on the mast. She stepped over to it and tentatively tapped the down arrow. The winch moved a bit before stopping. She pressed it again, this time holding the button down, but the winch jerked and whirred. He was clipped in, fastened to the mast. His body bucked upwards, pressing against the strapping on the bosun's chair, while the winch tried to pull him down. She took her finger off the button like she'd been burnt.

She sat back down on the bench.

'Jerry,' she whimpered. She knew it was pointless.

She looked up at the mast. It shook in a gust of wind. He can't stay up there, she thought, he mustn't. But she couldn't climb the mast with her hip and even if she could, it was sixty-foot up to unclip Jerry, followed by a sixty-foot climb down to press the button for the chair. And what would she do with him, even if she did get him down?

The waves below her churned white, pushed apart by

the boat's bow. Once the boat had cut through them, she watched them settle back into the roll and pull of the current, restored and in their element. Beyond them, the horizon dipped and rose.

It'll come later, the grief, she thought.

She went down to check the autopilot. The boat was moving towards the Caribbean. Jerry had typed their destination in the night before, 'Making the miles while we sleep.' He'd patted the control panel when it was done. 'That should see us straight. Three-week journey, wind and weather permitting. Part of the old Rally Route. Bloody marvellous.'

She sat down in front of the communications suite and studied the equipment. She'd walked past it countless times every trip, taking breakfast, lunch and dinner up on deck, and their gin and tonics and nibbles at 6pm. As she stared at the equipment, she was struck by the realisation that she couldn't ask Jerry to help. That he wouldn't walk past and say, 'Give it here, woman.'

She stood up and took a long breath.

'Come on, Anne,' she told herself, 'put your mind to it.'

She sat back down in the chair and concentrated on the technology.

She played around with the radio. It tuned into someone speaking in Spanish. Were they talking about the sea, she wondered? There was no panic in the voice, they were going about their daily business. 'Life goes on, duck,' as her mother said when they left her father's hospital room for the last time. She moved the radio on and it found some calypso music, with a man singing, '*Girl be smart, play your part...*' She left it playing, while she investigated the panel. After a few more songs, and a bit of trial and error, she remembered how the panel worked.

She climbed back on deck. He was still swaying from the mast. She had hoped for a moment that it had all been a mistake, that he'd somehow dozed off and was now sitting upright, administering to the electronics. Seeing her, he'd shout down, 'What's for lunch?' But he didn't. He remained slumped over in the chair, the back of his shirt flapping as the seat and mast rocked in the wind. She could see his calf poking out from under the khaki shorts and knew that the patch of psoriasis on his right shin would be facing the sun.

He felt a long way away up there, turned away from her.

A seagull landed on the railing just along from her, its pink feet gripped the boat whilst its wings settled into its large body. It cast its pale, orange rimmed eye sharply across the deck.

Its body was still but the eyes and head were alert and alive.

'Hello Mr Gully Gully. I've got nothing for you to eat up here, I'm afraid.'

The bird walked up and down the railing.

'Where are all your friends? Are you lost?'

She paused but the bird made no noise.

'That's my Jerry up there. Can you see him? We've been married fifty years. Have you come to keep me company? If you stay, I'll go and get you something to eat. Will you wait? If I give you some nice food, will you take a message to Rachel for me? To ask her if Yusef would mind me coming to the Blue Mosque with them?'

It was just after the final argument with Rachel, that the stories in the papers started.

The Knight, the Swiss and the billion-dollar Ponzi scheme, was the headline in *The Guardian*.

'You don't need to worry about it,' he'd told her. 'It's press nonsense.'

He would say no more about it, but she read all the stories and followed the coverage online.

'They don't know what they're bloody talking about. And since when have you shown the slightest bit of interest in my work, anyway?' he snapped.

She read about the settlement in the paper. US$ 137 million. *ACC Group did not file a defence.*

'He's a criminal, mum,' said Rachel on the phone.

'Oh, I'm sure he's not,' she'd replied. 'And you mustn't say that about your father.'

She asked him about it that night.

'If I'd have done anything wrong, they'd have taken my knighthood away, wouldn't they? Now, let's bloody drop it.'

She told her mother all about it when she visited her in hospital. By that stage, she could only repeat, 'I feel so dopey. I feel so dopey,' over and over again. Anne talked alongside her in a whisper, telling her all the things she'd read in the papers. She knew what her mother would say, if she could. 'Your ship's come in, duck. And there's you now, with everything you could ever want. You hang on to him. And be sure to have your make-up on when he gets home from work. There are women in that office you know. You're not so special, duck.'

Anne didn't bother telling her mother about Rachel. She knew what her view would be on a man called Yusef.

'Not PLU,' Jerry had said after Rachel and Yusef's first visit. 'Anyway, it won't last. It can't last. She can't live her life like it's a bloody Beach Bar in Turkey.'

In those months after Rachel returned from travelling, Anne watched him as he railed at this 'ridiculous bloody thing,' worrying at it, unable to grasp it.

'I just don't know what she's thinking. I don't think she *is* thinking!'

Until the night Rachel and Yusef stayed over, and he said those things he shouldn't have said.

Anne cried when Rachel told her they wouldn't visit anymore.

'I've got to stand by your dad, but you know I don't agree with him about you and Yusef.'

When she told Jerry, he shook his head and shouted, 'Am I the only one who knows what the bloody Turk's up to?'

Anne was scattering some crisps for the seagull when she heard the voices from the communications panel.

'Hello, Sir Jeremy? Can you hear us, Commodore? It's David and Roger, reporting for duty, sir.' She heard the two men laugh. 'Just wondering how you and Lady Crawford are getting on? We're having a fine old time. Weather's wonderful, isn't it? Perfect sailing conditions. Still waiting for the wives to surface from the drinks' cabinet, but what can you expect?' The men guffawed again. 'Well, keep the lines of communication open. Look forward to hearing from you soon, Commodore. Over and Out.'

Anne listened from the steps. As they signed off, she sighed. She thought about all the people at the Sailing Club. The people at his work. Their friends. All those people she would have to tell. All those conversations. All those arrangements to be made. She felt the weight, hanging over her. She looked out at the sea, surrounding her, protecting her. It could wait. She would decide when to start it. She threw more crisps for the bird.

'Will Rachel come to the funeral, Mr Gully Gully?'

The bird hopped across the deck on its webbed feet. It stood over Jerry's skipper's cap. Anne moved towards it and the bird flew away. She picked the cap up. Stitched into the front in red lettering was,

Sir Jeremy Crawford
Club Commodore

She fingered the lettering, then spun the cap out into the ocean. It briefly lifted on the air, before settling onto the surface. The current pulled at it and as the boat moved on, she watched it disappear, submerged below the waves.

In bed that night, she listened to the autopilot, pushing her towards Antigua. The bed felt large and quiet. The sheets were cool on Jerry's side. She looked at the space next to her. She smelled his pillow. She'd always liked his smell. She lay looking at the cabin ceiling, remembering them arguing about whether Rachel and Yusef should share a room when they stayed over.

'Not under my bloody roof.'

But Anne had made up the spare room for them.

'She's an adult, Jerry.'

Then him coming to bed having walked in on them kissing in the kitchen.

'Does he have to rub my nose in it? They didn't even look embarrassed.'

'Oh, it's nice. They like each other.'

'And now we're going to have to listen to God knows what going on.'

'Oh, don't be ridiculous, Jerry. You won't hear anything, unless you go and stand outside their door.'

'I'm not a bloody pervert, Anne. It's just not what I wanted for her...'

'Well, don't you say anything.'

The following morning was very hot again. She wasn't looking forward to looking through the binoculars. She went to the front end of the boat to see his face better. She'd suggested he put sun cream on before he went up the mast, but he'd scoffed, 'I won't be up there a minute,' and now she could see that a full day in the 35 degrees sunshine and the night's winds, had left any exposed flesh burnt bright red and his forehead blistered. His eyes looked dull and crusty. His shirt was ripped, and she could see his exposed gut, glowing and angry.

She closed her eyes and thought of him as a young man. How handsome he was. But that was all finished now. All of Jerry was finished – young, middle aged, old, home, work, husband, father, son - and every single part of her life with Jerry was over.

She heard the radio.

'Hello. Hello. Sir Jeremy, are you there? It's David

Wilmslow, again. Please pick up, if you can hear me. I left a message last night. Not like you to not reply. Just checking all's okay. Please pick up if you can hear this.'

She picked up the controller.

'Hello David, this is Anne Crawford.'

'Ah, Lady Crawford. Hope all's well. I was hoping to speak to Sir Jeremy?'

'Jerry's dead, David.'

The radio fell silent.

'I think he had a heart attack.'

'Oh, good Lord... I'm so sorry. You must call in to the coastguard. I don't suppose you're familiar with the controls. You need to...'

'I know how to do it, David.'

'Oh, right.' He paused. 'I'll turn back immediately, then we'll pick you up on the radar. I'll speak to the coastguard. Shouldn't be more than three or four hours. Now, be sure to drink plenty of water and don't touch any of the equipment. I'll be there as soon as I can, Lady Crawford. Then you can have a good cry with Sandy and we'll get you home. Terrible business.'

'David.'

'Yes, Lady Crawford?'

'Please, call me Anne.'

After his voice shut off, she turned off the autopilot. The boat settled in the water. Her senses adjusted, freed from the constant thrum of the engine. She could hear the water lapping against the hull. The seagull squawked from the railing.

Only when she got back on deck did she realise that she'd

taken the steps like she used to, before the hip started to hurt, long before the operation. She looked towards the horizon. It moved with the boat, but she planted her feet and rolled with the motion, fixing her eyes on it. The water around the boat was turquoise green, but where she was looking it was deepest blue until it washed into the white of the horizon.

She removed her cover-up. The sun enveloped her body and she luxuriated in it. Closing her eyes, she turned her face to the sun. The warmth sank into her. She took a breath and held it in. After she exhaled, she climbed onto the bench and placed her feet on the side of the boat, her toes hooked over the top of the steps. She waited for her eyes to adjust after the sunshine.

The whole ocean lay before her.

She dived in.

All sound disappeared and the cold rushed over her. She opened her eyes into the blue, holding her breath as her body adjusted to the shock. She stayed under until she could push out her breath, watching it disturb the water in front of her, then shot to the surface, into the light. Her body felt electrified. She looked up at the sky and screamed. She threw her arms around, slapping the water's surface, then dipped back under before bursting up again. She floated on the surface and breathed deeply, suspended and cradled by the ocean.

The water dripped onto the deck. Her body was tingling. She removed her bikini. Top first, then bottoms. She looked down at her body, with its scars and red spots, its veins and faded stretch marks and felt the sun caress it. She lay down on the deck and let the sun dry her.

By the time she was helped onto *The Albion* by David Wilmslow, Anne was back in her linen trousers, a top and light cardigan and sun hat.

'I'd like to call Rachel, please,' was all she'd said as she stepped aboard and David had assured her this would be arranged as soon as they were underway.

'No, I'd like to call her now, please.'

Roger took the helm of *The Bonus*, whilst David stayed on *The Albion*, insisting that Sandy and Deborah stay below deck, for fear of exposing them to the sight of Sir Jeremy's battered and blistered corpse. The wind was up and the men could hear his body being thrown about in the bosun's chair, his shirt inflated like a sail. Anne watched them repeatedly glancing at the mast, despite themselves.

The seagull sat on top of *The Bonus*'s mast, a couple of feet away from Jerry's body. It looked around the boat and across the sea, then hopped onto Jerry's body and pulled at the shirt fabric. Anne watched it tug at the shirt before flying away with a strip of the pale blue cotton in its mouth.

David Wilmslow turned to see Lady Crawford waving at nothing in the sky and shook his head, fearful of what such an experience would have done to the woman.

John Budden, @JohnBudden14, is the author of *We Aim to Live*, a collection of short stories that features *A Place in the Sun*.

Waiting for the Light

by DP Dignam

The winter sun was rising over the mountain but the light was wrong. I wouldn't get the photograph I wanted. I needed the special light you get when the sky is clear and there is frost on the ground. I put the camera back into its case and folded the tripod.

I only photograph landscapes these days. I used to go to war zones and my pictures won awards. The money was good and I was getting lots of commissions. One assignment changed everything. I tell people I discovered something terrible on that trip. They assume I mean the mass graves and the mutilated bodies.

It was years ago but I can remember every detail. We were due to fly from a small airstrip a few hundred miles from the border. It was raining as we waited to board the plane. The wind was twisting the clouds into strange shapes over the control tower.

I was going to a civil war that had been dragging on for years. The world had lost interest in it. I was afraid my photographs wouldn't sell but Vicky Taylor from the aid agency promised there would be things too terrible to ignore. That was just what I wanted and she agreed to show me around.

It was a short flight and Vicky was waiting at the terminal building when I got off the plane. The city had changed hands numerous times and there had been a lot of killing. Now there were terrible stories about what was being done in the villages further down the valley. Everyone seemed to be on edge. The weather didn't help. It was the time of year when the desert wind blows towards the sea for month after month. The locals believe that it can affect the minds of people and animals.

I hadn't been there long enough to know if that was true but something else was worrying me. I was taking anti-malarial pills and I'd been warned about the side effects. It could be anything from intense dreams to hallucinations. I didn't have much choice about swallowing the pills. The local strain of malaria could be fatal. On the first night I had a weird dream about being on holiday. I was alone on a beach and when the tide went out it revealed a line of corpses playing volleyball in the surf.

The next morning Vicky showed me the local attractions. Down on the beach, a row of rotting bodies stuck out of the sand. They were tangled in an old fishing net and being eaten by the crabs. The incoming tide moved their limbs up and down as if they were trying to throw something over the net. It wasn't exactly like my dream but it was a little unsettling.

After that we went to the ruined cathedral. There was a pile of human bones behind the pulpit. No one knew which faction had done the killing. I noticed a piece of stained glass on the floor. It was the face of an angel from the window in one of the side altars. Vicky was a little shocked when I re-arranged the bones to get that fragment of stained glass into my shot. I tried to explain it was all to do with composition but she didn't seem to understand.

Later we went to a food hand-out at a warehouse in the port. I photographed a woman in a green dress holding the hand of a small boy. He was staring right into the lens and reaching towards me. As I was refocusing he grabbed a pen from my shirt pocket. It had my agency logo running along its side. The mother apologized and told him to hand it back. I had lots of those pens so I told him to keep it. Everyone smiled.

I snapped away for another few minutes but I was getting frustrated. I had taken some good pictures but it wasn't enough. I needed something more dramatic; something that would really get attention back home. The people at the hand-out were close to starvation but that wasn't good enough for the camera. They didn't yet have that hollowed out look of famine victims.

I went to bed early that evening but that desert wind kept me awake. It was still blowing towards the sea and I was starting to understand why the locals feared it. It was getting on my nerves. It seemed to scrape through the trees like the claws of an invisible predator. It never stopped.

When I finally fell asleep I had another of my strange dreams. I was alone on the beach again. Suddenly, the sand turned to copper and mechanical ants started swarming across it. The insects started moving towards me. I tried to run away but my legs were sinking into the ground. I woke up sweating and went to the water filter. After a few big gulps I lay down again and waited for the dawn. I didn't want to fall asleep again.

A couple of days later the army let me join one of their foot patrols. As we approached the centre of the city, I felt the surface of the road change. It was like walking on a shingle beach. When I looked down, I saw the road was covered with hundreds of copper cartridge cases. One of the soldiers told me there had been a big battle there and lots of machine gun fire. Insects were swarming over the spent cartridges looking for dried blood. I remembered my dream and the mechanical ants. It felt creepy but I kept taking my pictures. We got back to the compound late in the evening. I swallowed my pills and the last of my Scotch. I was really tired and I staggered off to bed and fell asleep.

The dreams started again. I was looking into my viewfinder photographing the woman in the green dress and her son. I was behind them but as I was framing a shot they turned to face me. Blood was spurting from their throats and splashing down onto their clothes.

The boy was pointing at me and suddenly he stepped forward and poked his bloody fingers into my camera. They passed through the lens and touched my eye. Somehow, I continued taking pictures but there was blood on the lens and I couldn't wipe it clean. My photographs were ruined. They were smeared with blood. It was still dark when I woke up. I was shaking. I took my camera out of the case to check that there was no blood on the lens. I felt stupid doing that. I knew it was just a dream but I couldn't help myself.

In the morning we heard that one of the army patrols had found another massacre site. They were claiming there were hundreds of corpses in a pit on the other side of town. I forgot about the dream. This was the big story I had been hoping for. Vicky drove me to the neighbourhood so I could photograph the bodies before they were buried. I soon realised it was going to be something special. We could smell the corpses the moment we stepped out of the car.

They hadn't been exaggerating about the number of dead. All of them had been hacked to death with machetes. I know it sounds strange but I couldn't think of them as people. Through the lens they seemed more like broken statues. I got down into the pit to shoot the bodies really close up. It was a little overcast but I was getting some great images.

Suddenly Vicky screamed. I didn't know what was wrong. She was pointing down at my shoes. I'd stepped onto a dead woman's face. She made me get out of the pit. I wasn't too put out. I knew I already had enough material to impress the picture editors in London.

Vicky asked me if I wanted to stay for the burials but I shook my head. The images of the bodies in the pit were right on the money. I was about to pack up when things got even better. The clouds parted and a shaft of sunlight fell onto the body of a young girl. Her hands were clasped together as if she had been praying when they butchered her. I snapped her from several angles. When I finally put away the camera Vicky bent down and picked up a pen. She looked at me and asked if it was mine. It was covered with blood but I could see the agency logo on it. It was the pen I had given to the little boy.

When they pulled some more bodies out of the pit I saw the remains of the woman in the green dress. Her son was lying beside her. Their throats had been cut. Of course, I took out the camera again but I wasn't feeling well. I slipped and my camera fell on the boy's body. There was blood on the lens when I picked it up. That really spooked me. I knew it was time to leave.

Vicky drove me back to the compound, but I found it hard to have a proper conversation with her. She was upset about the massacre. She had known some of the victims. I was still trying to make sense of my strange dreams. I kept telling myself that I had my pictures and that was all that mattered but I felt sick. Vicky asked me if I was alright. I told her the anti-malarial pills were making me unwell.

I managed to stay awake for the next couple of nights but I knew I couldn't keep going much longer. I was desperate to leave. I thought the massacre pictures were as good as it was going to get on the trip. I was relieved when Vicky said an aid plane was coming. She said she could get me on the flight out.

She was supposed to take me to the plane that afternoon but she was late. There had been some gunfire on the other side of the river and she had been forced to take a different road to the compound.

Vicky finally turned up and we set off. My camera with the telephoto lens was on my lap as we drove towards the airfield. I didn't think I needed any more pictures but I started taking shots through the open window. We were close to the airfield when I saw a woman lying in the grass about fifty yards from the road. I focused was my lens on her. The woman had suffered a fatal gunshot wound to her temple. A dark, red halo of congealed blood had formed around her head. There was a little bundle at her side and when I zoomed in I saw it contained a baby. The child's eyes stared back at me. I took several pictures but I didn't say anything to Vicky. I didn't want to miss the plane.

When it was time to say goodbye, I told Vicky about the dead woman and the baby. She looked shocked. She wanted to know why I hadn't asked her to stop the car. I didn't know what to say. She said she would try to find the baby on her way back to the city. I stepped onto the plane and slumped into a seat. The hum of the engines put me to sleep almost immediately and, of course, another dream started.

I was back in the car with Vicky, photographing the dead women by the airfield road. Her baby started crawling after us. No matter how fast we drove it still followed, getting closer all the time. Finally, the child was close enough to grab my camera strap and soon I was being pulled out of the car. Fortunately, the plane made a bumpy landing and it woke me up. I was sweating and short of breath. I tried to persuade myself that the dream meant nothing. I had gone there to take pictures. No one could expect me to rescue babies.

A few days later I was back in London. The massacre pictures were syndicated everywhere but the image of the dead woman lying with her baby on the airfield road was the most popular. I made a lot of money from that shot.

A couple of weeks after I returned home I called Vicky. I asked her if she had found the baby. She said she had searched the road but she hadn't seen any trace of the dead woman or her child. She said the airport road was quite busy and there was a good chance someone else had stopped to help.

Vicky asked me if I was feeling better and I reassured her that everything fine now I had stopped taking the anti-malaria pills. I couldn't tell her the truth. I was afraid she would think I was mad. My weird dreams haven't gone away. At first I wanted to believe there was nothing unusual about them. I told myself they were just a side-effect of the pills or maybe something to do with that desert wind. I try to be rational about things but the same nightmare returns most nights. I am driving along the airfield road and that baby is crawling after me.

As I said, I got big money offers to go to other war zones but I turned them down. People thought I had lost my nerve. Maybe this is true, but I wasn't worried about the bombs and the bullets. I discovered something terrible about myself on that last trip. That's why I'll be back on the mountain tomorrow waiting for the light. The forecast isn't good so I expect it will be another wasted dawn.

DP Dignam was an award winning journalist at a major international news organisation for many years. Recently he has focused on writing short fiction. He has just finished a novel for children which will soon be ready for submission to agents and publishers.

I Used To Live Here Once

by MS Clary

'That woman was here again today.'

'Woman?'

'That one you thought came to collect for Donkeys?'

Raymond thought his wife wasn't looking her best. Looked like she could do with a bit of chicken. How about an eat-all-you-want-buffet for ten pounds tomorrow night was on the tip of his tongue.

'I hope you didn't give her anything.'

Sandra was peeling an onion. 'She wasn't collecting for donkeys.'

'What was it then, llamas?'

'She says she was born in this house.'

'So?' He started for the door, assuming the conversation had ended. The smell of frying onions began to fill the kitchen.

'I told her to come back in the morning and she could have a look around.'

Raymond paused. 'I don't like the idea of a stranger looking round our house,' he said.

'So you'll need to take those engine parts out of the spare bedroom.'

'Where am I supposed to put them?' he grumbled.

'This won't be ready for half an hour, so you've plenty of time.'

'Why does she need to see the spare room anyway?'

'That's where she was conceived,' she replied, starting on the cabbage.

Saturday morning they woke to a sky heavy with rain. Sandra put out the second-best mugs and a packet of hobnobs. At precisely eleven o'clock the bell rang. On the doorstep stood a stout middle-aged woman in a raincoat holding a bunch of flowers.

'I'm Rosalind,' said the woman. 'These are for you.'

'Chrysanthemums,' said Sandra, noting drooping petals already turning brown. 'How thoughtful.'

'It's all I could find.'

'Lovely,' she said juggling the flowers. 'Do come in. I'll put these in water...'

The woman ignored her outstretched hand and walked past her down the hall to the kitchen. She clearly knew her way around.

'I expect it's changed a lot since you lived here,' said Sandra searching for a vase. Why is it you can never find the right vase? 'My husband Raymond built the extension himself.'

'Vandals,' muttered Rosalind. Sandra thought she must have misheard.

The woman turned and swept into the lounge. Sandra,

unable to find the right container, left the flowers on the draining board and followed. 'We knocked these two rooms together,' she explained, 'to give us more space. Was this where you did your homework?'

'Wicked,' muttered Rosalind.

'I'll call my husband,' said Sandra, confused. 'He's in the shed. These men and their sheds...' Ray entered the room, a whiff of engine oil clinging to his denims. He was not happy. It had poured overnight and the shed roof leaked.

Sandra felt uneasy. She hoped Rosalind might say something pleasant to Ray about the extension that had taken him two years to finish, but she was staring out of the French window.

'What's happened to the sycamore?'

'There was no sycamore when we moved in,' replied Sandra. 'We put in the decking and the acer,' she offered.

'Vandals,' the woman muttered again.

This time Sandra knew she'd heard correctly.

'Would you like to see upstairs now?' she asked.

The woman stared past her. 'I don't think so.'

All that effort to rearrange the spare room and she wasn't even interested. Ray had been right all along. This was a big mistake.

'We used to have bookcases in here,' said the woman. 'Daddy was an intellectual.'

'That's a shame' said Sandra. What else could she say?

'Daddy was a very special man. Of course, so was Mummy.'

Sandra wondered if that's how her children would have

described her and Ray if they'd been blessed. Perhaps not the intellectual bit.

'Where's the standard lamp?' Rosalind continued.

The woman's lost it, thought Sandra. We should get rid of her quickly. She glanced to Ray for support but he had already gone back outside. The rain continued to fall. Rosalind strode back to the hall. 'I've seen enough,' she said, walking to the front door, opening it and slamming it shut behind her.

Not even a Thank You, thought Sandra, seriously ruffled. Ray found her in the kitchen, her head bent over *World of Interiors*, nibbling a biscuit.

'Well, that went well,' he observed.

'Don't start.'

'Who did she think she is?' asked Ray. 'Acting as if she still lived here. What did she think of the spare room?'

'We never got that far. She acted so strange.'

'There's rain fell all over the bike.'

'You need to fix that shed roof. Have a hobnob.' She picked up the chrysanthemums and tossed them into the bin. The lid snapped shut.

Sandra had set aside Sunday morning to clear the hall and study some colour charts. They were freshening up, as she liked to call it.

'I favour the grey,' she said.

He eyed her as she bent over in her baggy dungarees and wondered if he could suggest going back to bed for an hour.

'But perhaps Ghostly Whispers is a bit too pale?'

Ray was happy to leave such decisions to his wife. They had agreed he would spend a half hour testing his bargain recycled tyres while she cleared out the hall cupboard. Outside the wind was gusting, falling leaves down the street and into the gutters. She was deliberating the fate of a pair of Ray's old trainers when the doorbell rang. A young man stood on the doorstep.

'I'm sorry I have no need of more dusters.'

He held out his hand. 'I'm Ralph, Ralph Harris.'

She took in his shiny brown shoes and thought the name sounded familiar.

'I think you met my mother. You kindly let her look round your house.'

Sandra hoped he didn't want to look round too. 'I'm a bit busy at the minute,' she said.

'I'm sorry to trouble you, but my mother left her bag behind.'

Sandra frowned. 'No, I don't think so. I've found nothing.'

He was glancing past her as she spoke, as if expecting to see his mother's bag among the old magazines and broken umbrellas.

'She had it with her when you went upstairs.'

'We never went upstairs,' said Sandra.

Sandra didn't like the way the conversation was going and was relieved to hear the sound of Ray's bike blasting down the street. 'My husband's here now,' she said.

'Ray. This is Rosalind's son. Rosalind,' she said with emphasis, 'who came here yesterday.'

Ray, sensing trouble, removed his helmet.

'Rosalind says she left her bag behind. Ralph's come to collect it.'

'Well give it to him, then.'

'The point is, the bag's not here, she didn't go upstairs.'

'No. She never went upstairs.'

'See?' Said Sandra triumphantly. 'My husband agrees. She must have left it somewhere else.'

There was a short silence and for a moment she thought Ralph was going to argue.

'Sorry to bother you then,' he said, turning.

'Tell her to look in the last place she saw it,' Sandra called out helpfully as he walked away down the path.

'Well, the cheek of those two,' said Ray. 'You didn't find her bag, did you?'

'Of course not! The whole thing has been ridiculous from start to finish. I wish I'd never asked her in.'

'Those new tyres are no good,' said Ray. 'I'll have to get back to Eddie. What time's lunch?'

'I wasn't planning on lunch,' she replied.

She looked around, trying to remember where Rosalind had stood. Some of her hurtful words came back, but nothing looked out of place. Satisfied and about to leave the room, she glanced behind the sofa and saw a grey cloth shopping bag bearing the logo *Go With Flo*.

'All I can say is, Ray, it wasn't here yesterday.'

Ray ran to the front door and looked down the empty street. The strengthening wind sent a clutch of leaves into the hall. He came back shaking his head.

'No sign of him. What are you doing?'

Sandra was looking in the bag. 'There might be some identification,' she said.

They saw a large crumpled brown envelope held loosely together with parcel tape and an elastic band. As Sandra pulled it out, a large number of fifty pound notes fell onto the carpet. Ray knelt and swiftly tried to calculate, but stopped at nine hundred. Both sensed the heady, unfamiliar thrill of finding themselves in proximity to a large sum of money.

'There's a lot here,' he said faintly.

'We'll have to go to the police,' said Sandra

Ray was having difficulty articulating his thoughts.

'People don't usually carry that sort of amount around with them,' said Sandra.

'Unless they've robbed a bank. Suppose it's not above board. And why did she send that man to pick it up?'

'That's for the police to decide.'

Together, they carried on counting, putting the money into separate piles of five hundreds. It soon spread across the floor. When they'd finished, they counted again and agreed the sum came to just over nine thousand pounds. The notes had begun to topple and merge, so they stuffed them back into the bag, not bothering with the envelope. It took longer to replace them than it had to tip them out. Exhausted by the effort, they sat back on the sofa, eyes drawn, as if hypnotised, to the bag which seemed to have doubled in size.

'Do you think it's legal?' asked Sandra.

'Probably not. Let's not be hasty,' said Ray. 'She might come back. We don't need to get involved in something... you know...'

Sandra nodded. Cradling the bag as though it were a newborn, she carried it upstairs, pushed it to the back of her wardrobe and covered it with a skirt. In case somebody breaks in overnight, was her silent reply to Ray's unspoken question.

Ray slept well, despite the roar of Storm Brenda battering the trees against the windows. Sandra woke several times in the night. Once she fancied she heard the stairs creak. Later, she saw Rosalind climbing into the wardrobe. She knew she was dreaming, but was glad of Ray's comforting bulk beside her.

Next morning they woke to the persistent tip-tap of dripping water coming from the spare bedroom. They placed a couple of buckets and a saucepan under the leak. A brown stain was already forming on the ceiling.

Rob the roofer was up on the roof for at least ten minutes. 'Storm damage,' he confirmed. Several tiles cracked and a few dislodged. It would cost around fifteen hundred to fix. He had a lot on but would prioritise for a mate. What's more, he could start immediately. He added casually that for cash, he needn't charge VAT and he'd like an advance to cover materials.

Ray and Sandra looked at each other. This is an emergency, they said. Ray went to the wardrobe, opened the cloth bag and withdrew nine hundred pounds. For an extra couple of hundred, Rob would make good the damaged ceiling and help them lift the ruined carpet. His brother Bob could get them a lovely wool tufted at a special price.

A few weeks later, the work complete, they stood in the doorway admiring the finished effect.

'I think this room needs something, Ray.'

'It's just been painted, Sandra.'

'These mattresses must be ten years old.'

Only that morning, by chance, a flyer had come through the door advertising a sale at Wiggins, their local department store. They decided to treat themselves to a spot of lunch and a quick look in the furniture section. Once or twice, over lunch, their eyes met, aware what the other was thinking. Sandra voiced it first.

'What are we doing, Ray?'

'Having a nice lunch. How's your chicken?'

'You know what I mean.'

'All that cash lying around just encourages burglars.'

'What if they go to the police?'

'We'd have heard by now. Why didn't they come back? If anything's ever said, we'll pay it back. Or say we never found nothing.'

Sandra went cold as she felt a shadowy presence at her left shoulder, but it was only the waiter asking if everything was alright. They ordered another bottle of Prosecco.

'Drink up,' said Ray. 'Wiggins closes at five.'

Christmas could be difficult for Ray and Sandra with no children to visit or grandchildren to entertain. Sometimes they went to friends, but this year the friends were away.

'Can't we go away somewhere?' asked Sandra. 'What about a cruise?'

Ray pondered. He'd always been wary of water.

'We could go to the Med. See the Canaries.' She showed him the brochure that had come that morning.

'The ship leaves Southampton on the 23rd. It's been reduced to nine-fifty for the two of us.'

'Hmm.'

'Well, if you're not interested.'

'Don't be hasty.'

Sandra knew what Ray was thinking as he disappeared upstairs. He was in charge of Operation Wardrobe, as they called it.

'There's exactly seven thousand left,' he said, coming back into the room.

That settles it, thought Sandra, already online checking out details. The discussion had taken less than three minutes. The girl in the travel agency looked surprised when they offered payment in cash. They said they'd been saving up and had recently had a bit of luck on the horses. Their explanation was accepted without further comment. It's like having a secret bank account, thought Sandra. This is what life must be like for the rich. She recognised the girl slightly from Zumba.

From time to time, Sandra thought back to Ralph and the morning he had turned up at their door. But not often. As time went by, she found it easier to forget about him altogether. Though once, stopping to look at a particularly desirable pair of boots in a shop window, she caught him smiling back at her in the reflection. It felt like a sign of approval. He turned up unexpectedly in her favourite soap too, wearing his shiny shoes, so she stopped watching. She didn't tell Ray about these visitations.

They were pleasantly surprised to discover how many tradespeople and establishments welcomed cash payment. With a little judicious juggling, they were soon able to pay off their credit cards and no longer went over-drawn at the end of the month. Sandra could buy herself some little treats. They re-decorated the kitchen. Ray traded his bike and considered buying a car.

Sandra began to tell herself that Rosalind had deliberately left the money for them to find. Maybe she was dying and wanted the house returned to how she remembered it. The details were vague and didn't quite explain Ralph's turning up. Perhaps he was some kind of con-man. And why had they never come back to claim the money? None of it could be explained. It felt like an Act of God. Though she wasn't religious, she suggested trying a Service one Sunday but Ray poo-pooed the idea.

They hadn't kept all the money to themselves. There was the monthly donation to the Donkey Sanctuary. She hadn't hesitated to buy a set of tea towels and a duster she didn't need off the youth on a scheme, and she'd given generously to the Salvation Army before Christmas. The plaintive trumpet solo always brought a lump to her throat.

Sandra bought an evening dress for the cruise and some leather-soled sandals for dancing. Ray bought a suit. He'd never had a need to dress up so fancy before. Sandra felt proud as they strolled the decks in their new casual designer wear, exploring the ports and enjoying a champagne cocktail before dinner. It had been a wonderful holiday they agreed, as they clinked glasses on New Year's Eve with their new friends Sally and Pete from Kent. They promised to keep in touch when they returned to dry land.

One day in early spring, Sally invited them down for a weekend. Ray looked forward to trying out the new second hand BMW on the motorway.

After lunch in Pete and Sally's favourite restaurant, they strolled along the front. They sat for a while, looking out to sea, waiting for the iron man to gradually reappear as the tide went out. Sandra took deep breaths of the salty air, shielding her eyes from the glare, gazing towards the distant horizon. I don't think she will find me here, she thought, having recently spotted Rosalind in the vegetable aisle of the supermarket.

'This is Heaven, Ray. We could live here.'

Perhaps we could do with a change, thought Ray.

Walking back along Beach Avenue they passed a neat bungalow with a *For Sale* board outside. Sally and Pete knew the agent slightly and were encouraging. It seemed the owners wanted a quick move and they could view it the following morning.

'Oh Ray, this is perfect,' cried Sandra looking through the open window. 'Come and listen. I can hear the sea!'

They put their house on the market as soon as they got back. The next two months passed in a flurry of offers, counter offers, surveys and solicitors. While clearing out the wardrobe, Sandra came across an empty grey cloth bag. She held it out to Ray who, without comment, threw it into a plastic bag with the other rubbish. In late summer, they were able to move into the bungalow.

'Don't you think it was meant to be, Ray?' said Sandra, taking a breather before opening another box.

Ray, not wanting to tempt fate, just nodded.

The previous day he'd been tailed by a middle-aged woman who seemed to shadow his every step of the way home. He glanced round and quickened his pace as reached Beach Avenue but she was still behind him, closing the gap. His heart thumped so hard he thought it would leap out of his chest.

'Settling in?' called the woman cheerily as she passed him and waved before crossing the road. It had only been a friendly neighbour, but Ray didn't like the nervous twist in his stomach that stayed with him for most of the evening.

One afternoon in late autumn Pete and Sally informed them they were moving away to live near their daughter. They had a last farewell drink together, said their goodbyes and told each other they would be sure to keep in touch. We're going to miss them, they thought.

'Don't worry,' said Ray. 'We'll make new friends.'

Sandra pulled her jacket closer. The tide was high and a cool breeze had picked up. Oily dark waves splashed heavily against the sea wall.

'No sign of the iron man today,' she said.

'He'll be back tomorrow,' replied Ray.

They bought fish and chips and made their way home. It was already dark. They turned up the heating and were settling in for the evening when there was a knock at the door.

'I'll get it,' said Ray

At first he saw nobody. A full glittery moon cast its light across the street.

'There's nobody here,' he called, going to shut the door.

Two men stepped out from the shadows

'Who is it, Ray?' called Sandra.

One man took a step towards him. The other leaned lazily against the porch studying his nails. Ray shivered in the chill night air. He could hear the steady rumble of the shifting tide nearby, but it might have been traffic on the motorway.

'I've been expecting you,' he said. 'For a while now.'

He fancied he heard the sound of faint laughter and wasn't sure where it was coming from. It might have been his own. The moon had vanished behind the clouds. He wondered when he would see it again.

'Have you come to look around?'

'Very generous,' said one, as both men stepped forward.

'We used to live here once.'

MS CLARY was born in London. She studied Social Sciences at Manchester College Oxford, and LSE. She worked in the BBC, Social Services, and developed her own fashion business. She has won several prizes for short fiction and published two novels: *A Spell in France* (2017) and *Three Albert Terrace* (2022.) She's married with two sons and lives in Oxfordshire. www.msclary.co.uk

When we launched the competition in 2016, we received over 300 entries totalling 750,000 words. That's one and a half times the word count of *War & Peace*. Two of the winning stories were about refugees. 'Well, said one disgruntled entrant. 'All you have to do is write about refugees and Bob's your uncle.' Seven years later, I can happily confirm that *The Equalizer* and *Refuge* have both stood the test of time.

Each year, a dominant theme emerges. Infidelity, twins, dementia, revenge tales, dystopian societies... ghosts are always popular, especially ghosts who don't know they're ghosts. I was expecting a deluge of stories about Covid and lockdown in 2020 and 2021, but we received a couple at most. We get our fair share of what I term misery porn; stories in which dreadful things are described, often to children, but shock value is a poor trump card. The real aces are characterisation, atmosphere, structure, quality writing and sparkling but realistic dialogue, and many a good story has been spoilt by a poor ending.

Whittling down hundreds of stories to a shortlist is always a challenge. Every year, we appoint two independent readers, who read all stories anonymously. Around a month after the deadline, we settle down to some serious horse trading. Sometimes the readers are diametrically opposed. When this happens, the Marmite stories win over bland consensus any day.

As in life, luck plays its part. One year, the winning story made the shortlist only by a whisker. The two readers correctly guessed (by the writing style and the typeface) that two of their favourite stories were by the same author, and they decided to put only one of them forward in order to give another writer a chance. The winner will never know their luck.

Huge thanks to the authors who feature in this collection, all of whom have forfeited their royalties in favour of Chip-LitFest. Special mention to Rob McInroy, ringwoodpublishing.com, whose winning story *Burials* could not be featured, and to Helena Frith-Powell, whose story *The Japanese Gardener* had to be withdrawn from our shortlist as it was a Fish Prize winner.

We are incredibly grateful to HW Fisher, who sponsor the competition and also to our judges: Tessa Hadley, Martyn Waites, Rachel Seiffert, Sarah Franklin, Nicholas Royle, Isobel Dixon and Yasmin Kane.

A big thank you to all our volunteer readers (you know who you are!) for their passion and enthusiasm. Lastly, I would like to laud the hundreds of authors who have entered the competition over the years. Your tales have been a joy to read, and inevitably, some fabulous writing has remained unsung. Of the dozens of authors who have made our shortlist over the years, only two have done so twice, so please persevere. Long may we continue to receive your entries.

Catherine Evans
ChipLitFest Trustee & co-founder of Inkspot Publishing

Lightning Source UK Ltd.
Milton Keynes UK
UKHW011539250922
409421UK00002B/49

9 781739 630508